Devi's Game

Devi's Game

KEPLER-186F:
BOOK ONE

Alan Hamid

Alan Hamid

Contents

To Amie, my mom,
with love!

First print and ebook edition October 2023
Second print and ebook edition March 2024

ISBN: 978-1-7381812-3-0 (ebook)
ISBN: 978-1-7381812-2-3 (paperback)
ISBN: 978-1-7381812-1-6 (hardcover)

Reviews

Preface

Dear reader,

Thank you so much for choosing my debut novel, Devi's Game.

Kepler-186f is a trilogy, and Devi's Game is the first book in the series: an epic sci-fi fantasy.

Devi's Game follows the space odyssey of Geeta, a young, orphaned girl, from the valleys of Himalayas to an exoplanet, Kepler-186f, to build a fair and just world to save humanity at the brink of extinction. Geeta is a Dalit, a low caste.

Today, there are more than two hundred million Dalit people live in our world. For thousands of years, Dalits have been suffering discrimination based on their caste.

Still by many these human beings are considered as low caste and untouchable, only qualifying for the dirtiest jobs in the world. Experiencing violence, such as verbal and physical assaults, murders, and rapes, is a part of their daily lives. Geeta refuses to accept these societal norms and determined to create a fair and just world.

She wants to live in a world without any discrimination and have equal opportunity like any other human being. Little did she know that she will end up creating one on a distant exoplanet to save humanity.

Our planet is currently bruised and battered, but within, it still holds enough powers to heal itself, given no further damage is done to it. Racism is an extremely dangerous thing that could end humanity.

I pray that the day never comes when due to our mistakes, our children must leave Earth behind in search of an exoplanet like Kepler-186f for the sake of the survival of humanity.

I hope you enjoy this novel and help to build a better and just world, right here, on our beloved Planet Earth, for all of us who call it home.

Thank you,

Alan Hamid

The Author

Prologue

Dawn of Time

The origins of the war between the League of Gods and the malevolent Confederation's Dark Army remain shrouded in mystery, lost in the depths of time itself. It is a conflict that may have ignited since the birth of the universe, during the tumultuous period when galaxies were taking shape and cosmic forces were at play.

Throughout the vast expanse of galaxies, celestial entities aligned themselves with divergent allegiances, embodying the eternal struggle between good and evil. Some galaxies pledged their loyalty to the benevolent League of Gods, while others yielded to the dark allure of the Confederation. At the helm of this malevolent force was Lord Iblyse, the god of darkness, reigning over the Dark Planet.

Each deity brought unique strengths and perspectives to the cosmic stage, their ideologies converging in times of dire necessity as they faced the ruthless and evil Dark Army. Divine meetings were convened amid the celestial tapestry, leading to a fateful decision—the creation of a realm known as Earth. This realm would serve as a crucible where a hopeful species would evolve, becoming subjects for observation and experimentation.

Yet, within the intricate design of creation, Lord Iblyse

planted a nefarious seed that would later take form as Angahrie. She would become a harbinger of darkness, influencing the destiny of Earth in ways unforeseen by the divine councils.

***

In the year 2000 BCE, darkness blankets the Himalayan Forest where Angahrie's incarnation unfurls—from a massive hideous python into a seductive, gorgeous looking sorceress poised to wield wickedness.

As soon as Angahrie's transformation completed by the swamp, a witch emerged from the shadows and found refuge in the dark forest.

"Well, well, well," she began, "Look who finally decided to join the ranks of the sorceresses. Congratulations, Angahrie!

"Only took you a thousand years of servitude to Lord Iblyse to earn this reward, poor thing.

"But let me ask you, my dear, how long do you think this will last? Forever?"

The witch's cackle resonated through the swamp. Her lone eye fixated on Angahrie.

"What are you talking about, old hag?" Angahrie asked.

Drawing near, the witch's breath was hot and putrid as she leaned in.

"Oh, my dear Angahrie," she continued, "The prophecy."

Angahrie's eyes narrowed. "What prophecy?" she demanded.

The witch started whispering in Angahrie's ear.

The impact of the words was evident as Angahrie's face twisted into a mask of fury, her eyes blazing with infernal fire. Angahrie pressed for more information. "Who else knows about this?" she interrogated.

The witch, grinning maliciously, responded, "Only me, my dear. But don't worry, your secret is safe with me… at least for now."

Angahrie's beautiful features transformed grotesquely. Her neck distended, her mouth opened ten times wider than her skull, ready to engulf her next meal. In a sudden, predatory lunge, Angahrie trapped the unsuspecting witch, her serpentine instincts taking over.

The witch's body slowly disappeared into Angahrie's enormous serpentine jaw. As she went down through Angahrie's enlarged neck, the witch's silhouette fought desperately from within, her struggle futile against the crushing pressure; her bones snapped, a cacophony of pain and horror echoing through the swamp.

Angahrie's revulsion was obvious as she expelled the witch's single eye, a grotesque symbol of her conquest. Her forked tongue caressed her fangs, savoring the grisly feast.

***

Shortly thereafter, Angahrie ignited a colossal bonfire that cast eerie, flickering shadows across the desolate landscape. With a sinister purpose in mind, she reached down and clutched a decaying human skull, its eye sockets hollow. This vile relic of mortality seemed to pulse with an unnatural energy in her grasp.

Descending into the depths of a nearby pit, Angahrie unearthed a writhing mass of worms. These repugnant creatures squirmed in her hands, their hideous forms twisting and contorting. With malevolence gleaming in her eyes, she callously hurled them into the roaring flames of the bonfire.

As the worms met their fiery demise, the inferno erupted with a searing intensity. From the heart of the blaze, sparks danced like fiery specters, weaving and spiraling through the night air.

Gradually, these incandescent embers coalesced into ethereal female figures, their forms shifting and materializing with each flicker of the flames. They emerged as fearsome beings: like Amazonian warriors in stature and dreadfully beautiful.

These nightmarish entities, known as the Chingahries, numbered in the thousands, and congregated around Angahrie, their collective presence exuding an unholy aura.

As a relentless, nightmarish horde, the Chingahries yielded to their leader's commands. Guided by her dark intentions, they dispersed into the sprawling depths of the forest, their sinister mission clear: to infiltrate the highest echelons of human society and corrupt the minds of those in power, leaving a trail of darkness and despair in their wake.

Angahrie leading, the pack slithers into the shadows, bound together by their malevolent purpose. The birth of Angahrie marks only the inception of the darkness poised to engulf the world.

***

Stretching as far as the eye can see, a landscape of awe-inspiring grandeur unfolded, dominated by the ominous silhouette of a volcanic mountain. Jagged peaks pierced the heavens, their obsidian surfaces etched against the intense orange luminescence of molten lava cascading down the rugged slopes, during the night.

The mountain, a brooding titan, its stony visage marked by the ravages of countless eruptions.

Ashen remnants clung to its flanks, creating a contrast against the searing heat radiating from its heart.

The sky above was a sinister tapestry, cloaked in billowing clouds of ash and smoke. Erratic bursts of lightning intermittently illuminated the tableau, accentuating the raw potency of the volcanic forces at play.

Within this tumultuous tableau resided the lair of Angahrie, the embodiment of dark power.

***

In the dimly lit depths of a foreboding dungeon, Angahrie, shrouded in a robe of shadowy fabric, paced restlessly, her impatience palpable. The chamber was adorned with ancient tomes, skeletal remains, and enigmatic artifacts, their presence casting eerie silhouettes upon the cold, stone walls. The air itself was charged with arcane energies, a testament to Angahrie's mastery over the mystical.

As moments stretched into eternity, her impatience intensified. Fingers rhythmically drumming upon the armrest of her ornate throne, the sound reverberates through the chamber. Her incisive gaze swept the room, seeking signs of her trusted confidant, Sharara. A few other Chingahries, a dark assembly of resurrected serpent-women, stand as Angahrie's loyal acolytes.

Emerging from the shadows, Sharara stepped forth.

"Have you secured what I commanded?" Angahrie demanded.

With careful devotion, Sharara unveiled a small box clutched in her grasp. Angahrie leaned forward, her anticipation giving way to puzzlement, as she asked, "What is this? I required an entity resilient enough to survive even Earth's complete obliteration."

"Fear not," Sharara replied with pride, "It shall endure."

The faint trace of a grin upon Sharara's face suggested a profound assurance in her discovery. Angahrie's eyes widen in intrigue. Sharara assured Angahrie, "Its kind shall persevere when this world turns to dust."

Angahrie was still contemplating the specimen Sharara had found and asked, "And will this species assimilate the entirety of mankind's accrued knowledge over the forthcoming millennia?"

Sharara nodded.

"Very well," Angahrie replied. "Let us initiate the process of shaping the elite echelons of humanity's power structure, manipulating their very lineage across the span of ages."

Sharara provided more assurance. "Indeed. We shall imbue them with the wealth of knowledge mankind shall accrue. Their intellect shall rival, if not surpass, that of humans."

Drawing a deep breath, Angahrie's focus locked onto the enigmatic creature concealed within the box. She inquired, "What are they called?"

"This specific breed carries a unique label: Americano, commonly known as - cockroaches."

The cockroach within the confines of the box peered back at Angahrie with its massive eyes, a living testament to its endurance beyond her plot.

As Angahrie gazed upon the repulsive creature, her lips

curled into a sinister smile. With an authoritative tone, she commanded: "Commence the transmutation of these Americanos, infusing them with the cumulative wisdom of centuries.

"In time, they shall rise above humanity and assert their dominion over this world. And, when the time comes, they will be the only surviving species on the earth or shall we say on its bits and pieces."

Then, her attention shifted to the cockroach. "A Day shall come, a new era shall dawn, where earth shall be ruled by us: the cockroaches and the snakes."

A chilling, vicious laughter emanated from her, reverberating within the dungeon and beyond.

Lord Iblyse had incarnated this embodiment of the darkest evil across the cosmos, Angahrie, to carry out devil's work on Planet Earth. Her task was to subvert the gods' experiment.

***

Lord Iblyse, foreseeing events beyond the year 2200 A.D., devised a sinister contingency plan that aimed to obliterate Earth into cosmic fragments. This ominous strategy involved a missile like cataclysmic arsenal known as the Brimstones, each possessing a destructive power surpassing that of a million atomic bombs. Orchestrated by Lord Iblyse, the Brimstones were intended to shatter Earth into countless pieces, sending them hurtling beyond our solar system.

The success of this malicious plan hinged on Angahrie's involvement. Her task was to manipulate the genes of cockroaches and worms—Americanos and Chingahries—granting them the ability to assimilate human technological knowledge. In the aftermath of Earth's destruction, these creatures would regenerate amidst the ruins of nuclear wastelands, serving as a grotesque testament to Angahrie's hideous mind. In exchange for her services, Lord Iblyse promised her enhanced powers within the Confederation, on Dark Planet.

While the League of Gods remained occupied with fending off new massive black holes launched by Lord Iblyse, Angahrie operated covertly on Earth for nearly 4000 years. Collaborating with power-hungry and greedy humans, she corrupted their once-pure minds, making the planet increasingly fragile. By the time the League of Gods discovered her plan, it was tragically too late to avert the impending catastrophe, despite all their efforts and sacrifices.

The universe braced itself for the cataclysmic consequences of a plan that had been secretly unfolding for millennia.

1

Lotus

May 13, 1960, emerged as a day of unparalleled beauty. The sun ascended, casting its radiant embrace upon the Himalayan peaks, igniting a cascade of color throughout the valley. The lush flora and vibrant fauna danced in harmony.

Guiding young monks, brahmachari, in their tranquil morning stroll, the chants of the elder monks resonated with the serenity of dawn, each footfall a note that lifted the sun from the well of darkness, illuminating the world in its gentle embrace.

Their steps maintained a rhythm that harmonized with the very pulse of the universe. Their progress seemed like a collective effort to elevate the sun, to lift it from the abyss of darkness, ushering forth the light.

This serene journey came to a sudden halt with the wailing of a child. The monks' attentiveness shifted from their path to the cry, leading them to a humble bamboo hut – the dwelling of Pushpa.

Pushpa, a middle-aged Dalit woman of the untouchable caste, had dedicated her life to cleansing the village. Her lifeless form lay beside a fragile infant girl.

With unwavering compassion, they gathered the infant in their arms, returning to the temple to seek guidance from their high priest, Bapu.

***

Bapu, had been a high priest for half a century, possessed a demeanor marked by wisdom and kindness. Though he upheld the village's caste system, he grappled with its implications. He acknowledged the inherent injustices while maintaining the order he knew. His attitude towards the Dalit people, who were forbidden from the temple, was imbued with an underlying benevolence.

Bapu had just finished the cremation of Pushpa's body, and the monks convened in the temple's compound, seeking Bapu's guidance on the infant's fate. Bapu stood among them, his face a mask of contemplation as he observed the distant cremation.

In a voice gentle yet resolute, Bapu inquired, "Have we learned of the child's father?"

One of the senior brahmacharies spoke cautiously, the weight of his words evident, "Bapu, as you know, Pushpa had special friendships with several men in the village. It could be any one of them."

Bapu's raised hand silenced further speculation. "We cannot judge those who can no longer defend themselves," he said.

A younger brahmachari cast his gaze toward the cremation

site, and asked, "Bapu, what shall become of Pushpa's daughter?"

Bapu's eyes met the serene gaze of the infant, the child's eyes a pool of innocence. Bapu's soft voice held a tenderness, and a smile graced his lips, as if he foresaw the hope she would bring. "Take her to the Temple's Annath-Ashram, the orphanage. She will find refuge there," Bapu said in a calm tone.

The brahmacharies nodded in agreement. A teenage brahmachari voiced another question, "What shall we call her?"

Bapu's eyes rested on the child, a small smile forming at the corners of his mouth. He whispered the name, as if imparting a promise, "Geeta."

The newly born child passed from monk to monk, the very embodiment of hope amidst the world's shadows. While cruelty and darkness loomed beyond the temple's walls, within its embrace these monks held the power to nurture, to kindle a flame of love for those most in need.

Though the pyre's embers still glowed on the horizon, the monks directed their focus to the precious life cradled in their arms. In this moment, they embraced the promise of a brighter future.

From a knapsack, an elder monk produced a weathered ring, handing it to Bapu, "Bapu, this was on Pushpa's hand."

Bapu regarded the ring, his voice carrying the weight of remembrance, "I shall keep it for her and give it to her when she is old enough to wear it; a connection to her mother's memory, a beacon of her origins."

As the monks embarked on their journey to the Annath-Ashram, Geeta nestled within their midst. The Himalayan mountains basked in the sun's warm embrace. The sky stretched clear, and the gentle breeze seemed to harmonize with nature's song of welcome, celebrating the advent of a new life with a whispered Happy Birthday.

***

Geeta's village, Shanti, was something one would see in fairy tales, nestled in the peaks and valleys of the Himalayan Mountains. Shanti was located north of Kathmandu, somewhere in the Langtang region, close to Langtang Lirung Summit. It was a popular base camp for tourists and climbers to Mount Everest and other peaks, and home of some very experienced sherpas who guide the climbers.

The tranquil valleys held secrets that only the whispers of the wind could carry. Amidst this picturesque beauty lay the temple and its Annath-Ashram: a segregated orphanage, where caste dictated the path of destiny.

Geeta's existence began in the darkest corners of the orphanage. A world where birth determined one's fate. The very air she breathed seemed to carry the weight of tradition and prejudice.

From infancy, Geeta was relegated to a section reserved for the lowest caste, a silent reminder of her place in society. While privileged children savored indulgent meals and slept on comfortable beds, she ate plain rice and slept on the floor, but her spirit remained untouched by the limitations imposed upon her.

At four years old, she was entrusted with menial tasks,

deemed for her caste—collecting garbage on the streets of Shanti, and sweeping the dirt off the huge steps that lead to the temple. For another four years, she did it all with not only a smile but also with excellence. Her superiors promoted her.

Her new duties included collecting the shit of the village in a bamboo basket then carrying it over her head five miles away for while those of higher castes reveled in the joys of dance, music, and beauty.

Geeta's spirit was anything but resigned. With a heart that yearned for the forbidden, she dared to venture beyond the confines of her destiny and the village. Whenever she had free time, she would hide herself in the nearby forest. She forged friendships with creatures of elegance.

She would talk to birds, deer, and other creatures, as if they understood her language. Sometimes it appeared as if they were having conversations, as she would tell them her plans of finding her Rajkumar, a prince charming, and together they would change the horrible system of Shanti, so everyone treated fairly and live happily. All the creatures of the forest would chirp and nod as agreeing with her plans.

As Geeta matured into a teenager, the discrepancies became more evident. Yet, amidst her struggles, Geeta's curiosity knew no bounds. The years of hardship and discrimination only ignited a fire within her. She would conceal herself behind the walls of the higher-caste orphanage, absorbing the lessons of music and art, seemed like she was mimicking the lessons, learning new crafts. She would go to the forest and practice the skills she had learned, such a singing.

She would sing as loud as she could, as if she were some holy Imam in a mosque, calling the humanity to come and praise the Allah. And the creatures of the forest would answer the call and come to pray around her, as if she - standing tall amongst them - was their goddess: a Devi.

This talent would not only change her life, but also change the destiny of the world.

2

Girl of Substance

May 12, 1978, dawned as just another ordinary one for Geeta, who was on the brink of turning 18. If she did not have that shit load on her head and if she did not have to wear a ragtag saree made from discarded potato sacks, she would look like just another high school girl about to graduate.

The Himalayan Mountains greeted the sun's rays, as the dawn slowly lifted the vail off the scenic valley blossoming in the lush colors of spring. Geeta navigated the village with the bamboo basket, her burden a collection of filth from the community. Still, she found reason to smile – the paradise surrounding her Inspired her gratitude.

Then, it happened.

***

As Geeta approached the designated waste disposal site, an unexpected stumble sent her sprawling into a mess of human waste. It could be a fallen tree branch or a rock that might have tipped her over, but to her it felt like someone had pushed her really hard from her back.

The fecal matter clung to her, obscuring her face and body.

For a fleeting moment, she lay in the filth, weary and overwhelmed by the load she carried.

But then, a remarkable transformation took place. Instead of succumbing to despair, Geeta's frustration erupted into a scream of defiance as loud as her vocal cords would allow. Her shrieks echoed from the Himalaya Mountain as if they were about to shake up the whole world. With a surge of energy, she bolted towards a nearby river to plunge into its depths and end her miserable life.

***

After a short while, the bubbles that came to the surface due to her breathing, disappeared. The river became as still as it could be, without any sign of life. It appeared that she might have drowned herself.

Nobody knows what happened in the depths of those holy waters during those few quiet moments, but then, suddenly, Geeta's head emerged from the water desperate to get air in her lungs. She appeared transformed: Looking like a celestial being with radiated purity, wearing a smile that defied the trials she had endured.

Then, another scream came out of her that evolved into a song erupted from her lips, an anthem of resilience and revolt against her caste and destiny. Her voice rang out, an irresistible melody that beckoned the flora and fauna. Creatures of all kinds gathered at the riverbank, drawn by the ethereal harmony. The song was a celebration of fully recognizing the untapped powers within her and the sense of newfound freedom due to it: the song was a protest against the chains that bound her and a celebration of knowing the powers that lay within to break free.

***

Geeta's voice spilled like gentle rain over the entire village of Shanti. Her song summoned the villagers, urging them to join in the celebration of life's beauty. Her hymn called to the divine forces that governed the world, a thanksgiving for the breathtaking experience that their land provided.

As Geeta's voice filled the air, an unexpected transformation rippled through the village. Residents emerged from their homes, curious and intrigued by the extraordinary sound that had broken the usual morning silence. The melody compelled them to venture out, drawn towards its source.

Enchanted by her song, the villagers fell into steps behind her. With each stride she took, they found themselves confronting the biases that had shaped their judgements.

Yet, in their eyes, a flicker of doubt and unease lingered, as if they pondered whether the Gods might castigate them for their misjudgments – whether of Geeta's caste or of Geeta herself.

As Geeta sang, she walked through the cobblestone streets of Shanti, blissfully unaware of the crowd that had formed behind her. Her presence stirred awe and curiosity, her song captivating those who had never acknowledged her. She arrived at the temple steps, where Bapu stood, as if awaiting her.

Geeta stood there, unsure of what had come over her. The head monk's eyes met hers, admiration for her spirit evident in his gaze.

Bapu recognized the potential in Geeta's voice. The crowd that had gathered was unprecedented, an opportunity he could not overlook. Approaching her, he smiled, acknowledging her strength and the change she could bring about.

Curiosity and admiration danced in his eyes as he inquired, "Where did you learn to sing like that? Your voice… your words… simply beautiful. Unlike anything I've ever heard."

Bapu paused to reconsider what he was about to say. He continued, "Starting tomorrow, you will sing the morning prayer on the temple's steps. Your role has changed – no more waste collection."

With a gentle smile on his face, Bapu's gaze fixed upon Geeta.

Bapu hoped her voice could wake up Shanti every morning, and then, villagers could get closer to the source of the voice and come to the temple more often. Then, direly needed donations might go up.

Stunned, Geeta looked up to Bapu.

He nodded with a reassuring smile.

Geeta smiled back, and just as she was turned to leave, Bapu stopped her, "Wait!"

He went inside the temple, returning shortly thereafter, a nicely folded saree in his arms. There was also a weathered ring on the top of the brand-new saree.

"Tomorrow is your birthday, right? Here is a gift," said Bapu pointing to the ring. "This belongs to your mother, I kept it to give it to you, when you became old enough to wear it."

Geeta tried to hide her emotions with a smile of gratitude

and nodded her head acknowledging Bapu's offer and accepting it as if she really had a choice.

Geeta could not figure out how to response to this sudden change in her life and the new feeling of empowerment she was having. It was the first time she recognized the power within her of being capable to change her world on her own and had a better future for herself; little did she know that she was about to become the beacon, poised to rescue humanity from the brink of extinction.

Unsure how to react to all these new changes, while holding the saree and the ring, she quickly nodded to Bapu and ran off like a gazelle, trying to run back to the Himalayan Forest. She began to sing joyfully once more in celebration. Her voice was reaching the peaks of Himalayas and echoing all over Shanti and beyond.

***

Perhaps some of the sound waves of Geeta's heartfelt songs for a fair and just world eventually transcended the boundaries of the atmospheric barrier, perhaps reaching all the way to the distant Planet Kai-Nat, like a cosmic prayer.

There, the League of Gods was on the brink of convening to deliberate on a strategic decision that could potentially salvage their experimental creation, Planet Earth and the fragile human species inhabiting it.

3

Prelude to an Adventure

1979

In the timeless expanse of space and distant galaxies, the passage of time is elusive and unfathomable. However, in the context of Earth's reckoning, four thousand years had slipped away, marked by the clandestine spread of darkness orchestrated by Angahrie and Lord Iblyse. The fate of Earth seemed irrevocably sealed, succumbing to the insidious plan veiled in shadows.

As a final beacon of hope flickered in the face of impending doom, the League of Gods convened an urgent and vital meeting. In this crucial moment, two young and formidable champions, Dex and Talib, emerged as the chosen sons of the gods. Summoned to the emergency council, these adept gladiators held the potential to alter the course of destiny and confront the encroaching darkness.

Talib, born to the esteemed house of Lord Shakta on Planet Kai-Nat.

Lord Shakta was now a core figure in the League of Gods, presiding over its meetings as the head.

Dex, offspring of the mighty Lord Garaj from Planet Keh-Ka-Shan.

Lord Garaj possessed his own formidable powers, the most advanced arsenal in the battle against the Dark Army.

For two decades, the bond between Dex and Talib had been steadfast, a connection that transcended mere friendship. Born within moments of each other, they had navigated the tumultuous battlegrounds against the Dark Army, their camaraderie solidified through shared trials of fire and steel. As they reached the age of twenty, both Dex and Talib stood as formidable leaders, their equal qualifications positioning them as the rightful heirs poised to lead the League of Gods when the inevitable time arrived.

However, beneath their battle-hardened exteriors, a youthful exuberance still reigned. Their potential for leadership was unquestionable, yet their penchant for mischief and carefree living remained intact. The title of chairmanship might hold little interest for them; their friendship was the true treasure they prize above all else, a bond that seemed unbreakable until the fateful day they were summoned to Earth.

***

In the cosmic arena of Planet-Kai-Nat, Dex and Talib found themselves immersed in the exhilarating thrill of battle, facing off against ferocious dragons. The clash was fierce, with the last mighty dragon succumbing to their combined might, casting cinders and ashes upon the triumphant duo. The roaring crowd erupted into cheers for their favorite sons.

With a katana held like a samurai, Dex, and Talib, wielding a sword reminiscent of an Arab warrior from the Middle Ages, raised their weapons in acknowledgment of the crowd's adoration. Grinning like beacons, they embraced each other amid the jubilant cheers, sharing hearty pats on the back. However, their victorious moment was abruptly interrupted by a messenger bearing urgent summons.

The regal messenger sprinted towards the young men; his urgency evident. As he conveyed his message, he pinched his nose and took a few steps back. Talib and Dex exchanged glances before simultaneously bringing their armpits to their noses, catching a whiff of their post-dragon-fight aroma. The wrinkling of their noses and contorted expressions betrayed a shared sense of repulsion, as if the dragon's last breath lingered as a revengeful reminder from beyond the grave, threatening to induce nausea.

Having exchanged wry smiles at the olfactory aftermath of their victory, Dex and Talib sprang into action with lightning speed. Their destination: the parked flying pods at the far end of the arena. In the blink of an eye, they leaped into their vessels, leaving a trail of dust as they accelerated with blinding speed.

The passionate applause from the crowd served as a farewell salute, their adoration a testament to the spectacle Dex and Talib had provided. Responding with a wave of gratitude, they harnessed the power of their flying pods, streaking through the sky like celestial comets heading toward their destined destination—the headquarters.

***

Planet Kai-Nat, akin to Mercury in appearance, housed the illustrious headquarters of the League of Gods. The divine conference room within its heart bore witness to celestial deliberations of paramount import, seamlessly blending ancient majesty with futuristic marvels in an awe-inspiring synthesis. Marble columns reached skyward, intertwining with intricate murals depicting scenes from the cosmos. Golden light streamed through a colossal stained-glass dome, illuminating the polished marble floor in a dance of colors.

Holographic displays adorned its surface, showcasing galaxies and planetary systems, a tableau of the universe's intricate design. Within this ethereal enclave, the Divine Council assembled. Their presence exuded a grand fusion of power and wisdom as they gathered around an iridescent crystal table. If not for all the futuristic marvels and displays, this could be mistaken for an Emergency Special Session of the United Nations General Assembly.

At the heart of the chamber stood Lord Shakta, leader of the League of Gods, his commanding presence emanating ancient sagacity and boundless strength. He seemed a little impatient, looking at the entrance, waiting for Talib and Dex to arrive.

Shortly, Talib and Dex approached the entrance with their mechanical companions: Buddy and Dolly. Dolly, a robotic panda marvel, moved with graceful fluidity, while Buddy, a robotic camel masterpiece, scampered forward with uncontainable enthusiasm. These extraordinary creatures were the beloved companions of Dex and Talib, forming a bond that transcended the boundary between technology and companionship.

Swiftly, Talib and Dex approached the entrance, their mechanical companions, Buddy, and Dolly, in tow.

Dolly, the robotic female panda, moved with an animated and cheerful demeanor. Her mechanical limbs carried her with a delightful bounce, reminiscent of a playful panda frolicking in the bamboo forests. The movements were synchronized, creating an almost dance-like rhythm as she traversed the space, exuding a sense of happiness and whimsy.

Buddy, the robotic camel, size of a Great Dane, ambled along with a rhythmic gait, each step accompanied by a gentle swaying motion. As he walked, his mechanical jaws moved in a repetitive pattern, diligently chewing on a bundle of hay tied to his back.

The vibrant display of these two robotic marvels' joyful motions added a touch of animated liveliness to the surroundings. The act was oddly serene in the hallways of the gods, a fusion of artificial precision and natural grace, creating a unique and endearing spectacle. These extraordinary creatures held a cherished place in the hearts of Dex and Talib, their companionship transcending the conventional limits of technology and embracing the essence of genuine connection.

After sprucing up and donning elegant attire, the young men possessed a magnetic charm that could easily captivate any heart. They resembled recent high school graduates, with one striking exception in Dex's appearance: occasionally, his deep brown hair seemed to emit an unusual radiance, almost as if it had some highlights. This peculiarity stemmed from the unique nature of people from Planet Keh-Ka-Shan, whose hair reacted to their innermost emotions, effectively displaying their feelings for all to see.

Dex and Talib made gestures to have Buddy and Dolly seated next to the entrance, pointing to a sign, reading: *No Pets Allowed.*

The boys quickly walked, nodded to everyone in the room, and took their assigned seats. Lord Shakta acknowledged their arrival with a nod and started to speak in a voice that resonated with a symphony of authority and determination.

"Esteemed comrades, dire circumstances compel us to convene this emergency meeting," he began, his words flowing, each syllable commanding attention. "Our charges on Earth face an imminent threat. The vicious Lord Iblyse's most vile agent, Angahrie, has been spreading corruption among those in power for a while."

A ripple of concern traversed the assembly, each god's visage marked by the gravity of the situation.

Lord Garaj's voice came resolute. "Such a transgression is unacceptable! We must take swift action to rectify this situation."

Lord Shakta's words possessed the power to galvanize, his tone infused with both urgency and resolve.

"Prudence, dear friends," Lord Shakta advised. "Lord Iblyse is cunning and ruthless. We must tread carefully, unveiling the truth before we unleash our might." Lady Mohobut's thoughtful tone joined the discourse. "How might we uncover this truth, Lord Shakta?"

With wisdom and fondness in his eyes and a smile, Lord

Shakta looked towards Lady Mohobut, who had a flirtatious grin on her face. He replied to her, "The Oracle's visions have left no room for doubt. Angahrie, a malicious creation of Lord Iblyse, serves as his pawn in an unrelenting quest for dominion. The Oracle's insight warns that, should she succeed, Earth will be ruled by the mutated genes of snakes and cockroaches."

The assembly's apprehension deepened as the impending catastrophe took shape. Addressing them all, Lord Shakta continued: "However, if Angahrie fails, Lord Iblyse plans to unleash the deadliest arsenal, the Brimstones, upon Earth. He seeks humanity's extinction."

The Gods exchanged somber glances, their countenances a canvas of shared concern. Lord Shakta's stare shifted to Talib and Dex, the divine sons. Anticipation and unwavering determination etched across their youthful features, and their celestial heritage radiated from them. "Esteemed Lords and Ladies," Lord Shakta's voice resonated, "Our plan hinges on a delicate interplay between strength and empathy. Our divine children, Talib and Dex, possess exceptional skills and valor, but we must nurture another facet of their development."

All the heads turned towards the two young men, curiosity and intrigue kindled anew. "Compassion, empathy, and love are fundamental for guardians of humanity," Lord Shakta continued. "Talib and Dex must understand mortal struggles, connect with their emotions, and inspire humanity to transcend the darkness that befalls their world."

Representing Planet Hu-Soon, the younger-looking Lady Khoob-Sue-Rut's voice held a trace of uncertainty. "How can we ensure their success?"

Lord Shakta's gaze encompassed them all. "By immersing them in mortal lives, they will glean firsthand the value of compassion and love.

"This mission shall shape them into well-rounded champions, able to wield their godly powers while igniting humanity's hearts."

Talib and Dex exchanged resolute glances, their commitment unshaken. As Lord Shakta mentioned their names, they stood, embodying determination and readiness.

"Father, our hearts embrace this mission wholeheartedly," Talib vowed. "Acquiring these soft skills is vital to us. We shall not falter."

Dex's voice joined Talib's, an echo of resolve. "Indeed, Lord Shakta. We stand prepared for this journey, eager to learn and grow. The struggles of mortals shall become our own, and through our actions, we shall kindle light in their darkest hours."

The gods and goddesses rose from their seats. The faces of Talib and Dex gleamed. They could barely conceal their smiles.

The convergence ended as Lord Shakta's words resonated through the chamber, echoing in their hearts. The mission to Earth awaited them, and the destiny of gods and mortals hung in the balance.

***

Dex and Talib strode toward the gleaming spacecraft, christened the G.I.F.T., an acronym that stood for *Galactic Interstellar Frontier Transporter*. Its name was emblazoned on the metallic silver surface of the vessel, glistening as if inviting them to embark on an imminent space odyssey. The craft's engines hummed with potent energy, casting forth a mesmerizing play of azure and crimson lights.

The G.I.F.T. stood as a testament to divine craftsmanship, a celestial vehicle meticulously designed to harness the enigmatic power of the "Worm" and other interstellar phenomena, enabling journeys across the cosmos at speeds that defied the very concept of light. Through this ingenious fusion, distant galaxies could be traversed in the blink of an eye. Although a highly rare substance like dark matter, called MatterX, was required to leverage Traversable wormholes, called Bridges.

Its monumental metallic doors swung open, a grand gesture of welcome to its young commanders.

Just before they could board, a familiar friendly sound rang out. Dolly and Buddy hurtled toward them.

Like young Captain Kirk and Spock from Star Trek, Dex and Talib settled into their seats and issued commands like masters of their domain. Their instructions were directed towards Wisdom, an AI-powered quantum computing marvel, trained on billions of machine learning models nurtured on trillions of datapoints and an embodiment of the sheer potential of Artificial Intelligence.

Talib directed Wisdom, "Wisdom, commence the voyage to Planet Earth. Use Bridge."

From the depths of Wisdom's digital core, a melodious female voice emerged, its resonance seeming to ripple through the very fabric of space and time:

"Commencing the journey to Planet Earth.

"Getting authorization to use MatterX.

"Authorization granted.

"Estimated travel duration: 10 days.

"Arrival date on Earth: May 13, 1979, AD.

"Destination coordinates: The Himalayan Mountains Region. Close to Katmandu, Nepal."

4

Haré Rama Haré Krishna

A year had passed since Geeta was promoted to the role of the morning prayer singer. Every morning, before the sunrise, she would sing the prayers, standing outside on the huge steps of the temple; her serene melodious voice would resonate throughout Shanti as a wakeup call for the morning prayer, compelling people who were neglecting coming to the temple started a new routine. The once-empty temple steps transformed into a gathering place for people of all castes, united by the beauty of her song, a few inside and a lot outside the temple.

Each morning, villagers flocked to hear Geeta sing, drawn by the magnetic pull of her angelic voice. Her performances stirred something within them, causing them to question the long-held beliefs and prejudices that had divided their community for generations. Her influence wasn't confined to

32

Shanti alone. Travelers passing through caught wind of the captivating sound, and tales of Geeta's melodic voice spread to neighboring settlements. Outsiders and locals, both moved by her hidden messages in her songs and prayers and threatened by their potential to disrupt the established order, could not help but be affected by the echoes of her songs.

Amidst this shifting landscape, Bapu found himself at a crossroads. As the head monk of the temple, he had spent a lifetime upholding traditions. But Geeta's courage and the transformative power of her voice presented a dilemma he had not anticipated. He grappled with the responsibility of guiding his village through this time of transition while maintaining a delicate balance between the old and the new.

In the heart of Shanti, the temple became a hub of discussion and debate. Some celebrated Geeta's message of unity and progress, while others clung to the familiar comforts of the caste system. As the village experienced the ripples of change, tensions began to rise among those who had long benefited from the existing order.

Geeta's journey wasn't without its challenges. The same voice that inspired admiration also provoked adversity. A few questioned the audacity of a Dalit girl challenging the norms, while others saw her as a beacon of hope. Yet, no matter the response, Geeta remained steadfast, her spirit unwavering in the face of both support and resistance.

Geeta's path to empowerment took unexpected turns. As her fame spread, the village of Shanti began to transform in more ways than one. Visitors from neighboring countries,

Tibet, Nepal, and China started offering her tips and gifts as tokens of appreciation. With this newfound income, Geeta invested in herself and her dreams. She purchased a tape recorder and cassette player and began acquiring soundtracks of Bollywood movies. The rest of the funds were dedicated to bringing joy to the other Dalit children in the Annath-Ashram and the village itself.

Her generosity extended far beyond material possessions. Geeta frequently bestowed the children with the simple joys they had scarcely encountered—delighting in the shared bliss of ice cream and treats.

Every so often, Geeta would treat herself also. She became a big fan of Bollywood movies. Occasionally, she and her best friend, Asha, another Dalit girl, go to Katmandu to watch a matinee show and would return to village before sunset. They would purchase the cheapest tickets, sitting in the front rows on the floor, immersing themselves in the enchantment of new Bollywood films, especially those adorned with soundtracks that echoed the cadence of her heart.

It was on one such trip that Geeta's path took yet another unforeseen twist.

***

The sun's gentle embrace cast its morning glow upon Geeta as she completed her sacred prayer, standing outside, on the huge steps of the temple. Just as the tranquility of the moment settled, Asha burst in with the excitement of a child at play, waving a newspaper as though it held the key to their dreams.

"Geeta, look!" she exclaimed, her voice trilling with

enthusiasm. "Hare Rama Hare Krishna is finally playing at the Freak Street theater!"

Asha was more than just a friend to Geeta; she was a cherished companion, the one true confidante in her world. Hailing from the fringes of Shanti, Asha shared the same Dalit heritage as Geeta, a bond that had solidified over years of shared experiences. Their friendship had sprung from the roots of childhood, deepening with each passing day.

In Asha's parents, Geeta found a kind of affection that An-nath-Ashram couldn't provide—maternal and paternal love that embraced her as one of their own. Their gazes held the warmth of kinship, seeing Geeta not as an outsider, but as a daughter woven into the fabric of their lives.

Geeta's eyes lit up as she took the newspaper, her heart racing in synchrony with Asha's exhilaration. She scanned the movie times with quickening breath. "Hare Rama Hare Krishna! We been waiting to Katmandu forever!" she exclaimed, joy sparkling in her gaze. "The matinee starts at 2pm today. We must go, Asha."

Asha's laughter danced in the air, and she nodded with a sparkle in her eyes. "We'll be back well before sunset. We can't let this chance slip through our fingers."

Determination painted Geeta's expression. "We'll make it work," she vowed. "Meet me at the rickshaw stand in an hour?"

"Just let me get ready," Asha chimed, excitement bubbling within her.

They ran down the steps of the temple to get dressed for the occasion.

***

An hour later Geeta and Asha appeared at the rickshaw stand. Two young women looking like a vibrant embodiment of the counterculture era of 60s and 70s. Their attire held a touch of whimsy, echoing the bohemian spirit of the time. Geeta wore a flowing dress adorned with intricate paisley patterns, while the Asha sported flared jeans paired with a tie-dye shirt, exuding a laid-back yet fashionable vibe. Their laughter filled the rickshaw as they embarked on a journey toward the enchanting movie theater on Freak Street: Unaware of the fact that a shadowy presence loomed; an old 1967 Audi F trailing them like a predatory specter. Thakur Roy's ominous "Boys" occupied the car.

Much like her global strategy, Angahrie had orchestrated her network of operatives across the world, and Thakur Roy was the designated instrument to carry out Lord Iblyse's designs within Shanti. Operating as the puppeteer of Shanti, Thakur Roy thrived in the filthy underbelly of drug and human trafficking, ensnaring numerous vulnerable Dalit girls.

The rising prominence of Shanti, courtesy of Geeta's talent, struck a dissonant chord with Roy. The influx of attention from law enforcement and international figures grated on his nerves.

With meticulous calculation, Roy had hatched a plan to erase Geeta, mirroring the fate of countless girls before her. Whether vanishing into thin air or reeling from the horrors of rape and murder, the victims rarely saw justice served by the lethargic and corrupt local police. In this grim symphony of suffering, evidence often evaporated, leaving behind only insidious whispers before notifying any akin who might care.

***

Navigating the bustling streets of Kathmandu, the rickshaw carried Geeta and Asha with an air of excitement that was evident through their hushed conversations and infectious giggles. Amid the vivid surroundings, the theater's grand presence beckoned like a portal to enchantment, a haven from their unforgiving reality.

Inside the theater's embrace, emotions swirled freely. Laughter and tears intertwined with the tapestry of the on-screen narrative, a symphony of feelings that carried Geeta and Asha away on waves of storytelling and harmonious melodies. Each scene painted a canvas of emotions, and they surrendered to the enchantment of the theatrical journey.

When the final frames faded into credits, applause cascaded like rain. Geeta and Deepa emerged from the cinematic reverie, their spirits buoyed by the film's gift of optimism and metamorphosis.

Stepping onto the storied Freak Street, their minds still danced to the tunes of the movie, unaware of the sinister shadows lurking in the corners. In those obscure recesses, Roy's Boys laid in wait, cloaked in darkness, poised to execute their hideous plot.

5

Freak Street

In the heart of 1960s and 1970s Kathmandu, Nepal, Freak Street stood as a symbol of counter-cultural movement, drawing in a stream of free-spirited hippies and adventurous souls.

As Geeta and Asha strolled down the bustling thorough-fare of 1970s Kathmandu, the very air seemed alive with a kaleidoscope of sights and sounds. The vibrant Freak Street burst with energy. its sidewalks adorned with an array of shops and stalls that promised a journey of discovery.

The sidewalks were alive with the fervent pitches of street hawkers. Vibrant textiles draped the makeshift stands, their intricate patterns and vivid hues capturing the essence of Nepal's artistic heritage.

Among these treasures, Geeta and Asha found themselves pausing to appreciate the meticulously crafted jewelry that glistened beneath the warm sun, every bead and silver adorn-ment a testament to Nepal's rich craftsmanship.

Through the crowd, rickshaws and taxis navigated with practiced finesse, their drivers threading skillfully through the narrow street as pedestrians weaved between them. The rhythmic chime of rickshaw bells added a musical cadence to the lively panorama. Amidst snippets of conversation and the infectious laughter of passersby, the intoxicating aromas of local street food filled the air, drawing the senses with promises of culinary delights.

As Geeta and Asha walked, their conversation about Hare Rama Hare Krishna melded with the lively surroundings. The melodies from the film lingered on their lips, and they kept singing Dum Ma Ro, Dum, the tune that had nestled into their souls. Two young girls, poised to rewrite their destinies, immersed in a rare moment of joy, unaware of the threat: an old Audi trailing, its occupants, the predators, ready to strike.

In a heartbeat, the old Audi swooped in as the young women approach a corner, blocking their path.

Geeta and Asha clutched each other, narrowly escaping the car. Two of the predators, a tall and a short man, swiftly exited the vehicle and closed in on the girls, while the third remained behind the wheel.

With threatening intent, the short man, sneered in the local language, "Chokaries like you have no place here. Tainting even the movie theater seats, huh?"

The tall man's grip on Asha tightened.

Fueled by a mix of rage and fear, Geeta shot back, "Let go of her, or I'll scream for help!"

Scoffing laughter rang out, accompanied by chilling words of the tall man, "Who would risk their life for Achooth, untouchable, girls like you? Join us for some fun. Make a peep, and your throats will meet my blade."

Passersby averted their eyes, silent participants in this gruesome theatre. The injustice unfolded like clockwork; a daily reality hidden in plain sight.

Geeta's desperate cries filled the air. With her heart racing, she yelled, "Help! Anyone, please, help us!"

Pistols drawn, the predators aimed at the gathering crowd across the street, freezing them. The fate that awaited these young women was the same as so many others: abduction, rape, murder. Their bodies abandoned like refuse, destined for discovery. The municipality's workers would gather them, perhaps tampering with evidence before their families even knew. The truth obliterated. This brutal cycle passed down through generations.

In an instant, one of the men closed in on Geeta, while his partner held Asha captive. The chloroform-soaked rags emerged, despite the girls' valiant struggle. Geeta's pleas for help dwindled as unconsciousness overtook her, her cries fading into the abyss.

In the midst of this chaos, the waiting Audi swallowing the girls and their tormentors whole. The engine roared to life, a cloud of dust marking the car's escape. The desperate cries for help dissolved into the distance, the audience dispersing, the grim performance coming to an end.

Indifference reclaimed its throne, life resuming its rhythm, and the enigmatic streets of Freak Street absorbed the secrets, shrouded by the cold shadow of a society steeped in darkness.

Amidst the shifting crowd on Freak Street, a sudden gap

emerged, exposing the figures of Talib and Dex, who had arrived last night in Kathmandu in covert forms.

The two young men exuded a vibrant aura of the 70s, their attire a vivid reflection of the era's distinctive fashion. The air carried a hint of their curious exploration, embodying the spirit of the era's hippies. Bags slung over their shoulders concealed their weapons: the sword and the katana. Their gazes remained neutral, absorbing the scene before them. Then, Talib and Dex's eyes met, a silent exchange passing between them.

In a cacophony of tires against the road, the Audi hurtled through the twisting labyrinth of Kathmandu's narrow streets.

***

Unbeknownst to the driver and passenger, perched atop the car's roof were two unexpected passengers - Talib and Dex. They crouched as the cityscape gave way to hilly roads, the foliage brushing against the car's sides.

After a while, an unsettling shroud seemed to envelop the vehicle, its progress remaining stagnant despite the speedometer's steadfast indication of 65 MPH. Then, as if defying the laws of physics, the car defied gravity itself, ascending toward the canopy of trees.

A shared sense of astonishment washed over the occupants; their hands released their grips on their captives. With synchronized motion, the car doors swung open, revealing faces etched with confusion and awe.

In a swift, coordinated motion, Talib and Dex effortlessly extracted the predators from the car, the impact sending them sprawling to the ground. As the dust settled, the car gently descended back to earth, its tires making contact with the pavement once again.

With an air of calm authority, Talib and Dex observed the fleeing Roy's Boys, their initial audacity replaced by panicked retreat. But then in a blink, Talib and Dex stood before the would-be escapees, effectively cutting off their route. The predators' bravado had transformed into a desperate plea, their hands clasped together in an involuntary gesture of supplication.

Geeta's consciousness stirred like ripples in water. Urgently, she shook her friend. "Asha, wake up! Asha!"

Asha's groans marked her return to the realm of the aware, her senses grappling with the disorienting chaos around them.

Geeta cut through the confusion, her words a lifeline. "Asha, can you drive? Do you remember how? We need to escape, now!"

Asha nodded, her eyes struggling to focus on the disconcerting scene before her.

She found herself in the driver's seat, grappling with the dissonance between her groggy state and the urgent task at hand. Her foot slammed onto the gas pedal, and the old car hesitated for a moment before jolting forward, the wheels kicking up a swirling cloud of dust in its wake.

Geeta turned her head to capture a final glimpse of the two mysterious saviors through the rear window. Two odd looking hippies, one stood with a triumphant grin, while the other maintained his firm grip on the thwarted assailants. The car snaked around a bend, taking with it, Geeta's tangible connection to Talib and Dex. Their heroic intervention was etched into her memory, a beacon of hope in the darkness.

However, Asha's faculties were still ensnared by the lingering effects of the chloroform, her eyes fighting a battle to remain open. The narrow, serpentine road ahead presented a daunting challenge, one that seemed almost insurmountable in her hazy state.

As the car neared a sharp bend, Asha's grasp on control faltered, and the vehicle lurched, rolling down into a ditch.

With a jarring impact, the car came to a halt, its collision with a tree sending shockwaves through its occupants. Asha's head bore the brunt of the impact as it collided with the steering wheel, while Geeta was forcefully propelled through the shattered windshield.

***

In the aftermath, Geeta's semi-conscious form lay sprawled near the tree, her breathing labored and her movements feeble, a stream of blood coming down from the right side of her forehead. Asha, though not as severely hurt, managed to extricate herself from the wreckage and make her way to Geeta, her own pain momentarily eclipsed by concern for her friend.

Yet, as Asha drew near, an expression of sheer terror contorted Geeta's features. Her eyes widened as if sighting a ghost or some monster lurking just behind Asha.

"No, please no... she's my friend, my only friend..."

Unable to figure out who Geeta was talking to, Asha halted in her tracks, a mixture of confusion and concern clouding her expression. She turned around and did not see anyone or anything.

For a fleeting moment, Asha considered the possibility that the impact had jolted Geeta's senses or induced hallucinations.

"Geeta, it's me, Asha," she began to say, aiming to reassure and anchor her friend's fraying grasp on reality.

Just then an invisible force seized Asha from behind, lifting her from the ground. It tossed her into the tree like a rag doll. The sickening crack of her neck breaking sliced through the air, her wide eyes locked in a final expression of terror and disbelief.

Geeta screamed with anger and sadness.

The ring on her finger, given to her by Bapu as her mother's relic, began to emanate a radiant light: a surreal red glow was emerging from the ring, started to engulf Geeta, and she disappeared into it, leaving the body of her beloved friend behind.

6

First Dawn

Beside a serene pond adorned with vibrant lotus flowers and delicate water lilies, Bapu sat in serene contemplation. Graceful swans glided across the water's surface, weaving an elegant dance in harmony with the tranquility of the moment. Around him, young monks assembled in a peaceful circle, enveloped in a Zen-like atmosphere. Rows of oil lanterns emitted gentle, flickering light, casting a warm glow that bathed the gathering in a soft radiance.

In a voice that echoed with wisdom and compassion, Bapu began to speak, each word like a soothing balm for the soul.

"Love, my dear children, is the most potent force in our world.

"It unites hearts, fostering understanding and empathy among us all. With love, our hearts bloom with compassion and joy, shaping us into beings of divine expression. Without it, we remain adrift, set apart from the harmony that connects all life."

A monk named Ram rushed into the temple and waited for Bapu to acknowledge his presence. Bapu paused, looked at Ram, and nodded.

Taking the cue, Ram announced in a hurry, "Bapu, we have visitors in the village. Strangers seeking shelter before their climb of the Himalaya. They're searching for a Sherpa to guide them and a crew for their climb."

"Bring them here," Bapu replied, unruffled.

Moments later, two hippies entered the temple, with the satchels on their shoulders. They offered respectful bows to Bapu.

The elder's keen gaze discerned more than the eye could see, noting the sword and katana concealed within the travelers' bags.

One of them introduced himself and his companion.

"Greetings, revered Bapu. I am Talib, and this is my friend, Dex." A subtle nod from Dex acknowledged the spiritual presence around them. Talib continued,

"We seek lodging for a time, and we are prepared to offer generous compensation in return."

"Welcome to Shanti," Bapu replied. He then addresses another monk. "Ravi, please extend your gracious hospitality to our new guests. Lead them to the East quarter and ensure their comfort."

Bapu's gaze returned to Talib and Dex, his words a reflection of Shanti's philosophy.

"In our haven of Shanti, we do not seek payment for our hospitality. We believe that the arrival of guests is a divine blessing, a gift from the gods themselves."

A quick, shared smile between Talib and Dex captured the spirit of their encounter with Bapu.

With an inviting gesture, Bapu pointed toward Ravi, inviting the newcomers to follow. As they began to move, Talib patted Dex on his butt, eliciting gasps of shock from the observing monks. Whispers spread through the gathering, exchanging suspicious glances.

Standing next to the exit, two elderly monks in their eighties, covered their mouth with their hands, looked at each other in shock, and exchanged startled words in their native tongue. Translation of their conversation conveyed their bemusement. "Did you see that?" asked one old monk.

"They're very strange!", replied the other.

As Talib and Dex followed Ravi's lead, the ripples of their presence extended far beyond Shanti's walls. None of them knew at that moment that the destinies of not only Shanti but all of Earth were about to be reshaped.

***

In the hushed moments just before dawn, the temple emerged from the shroud of thick fog, a solemn sentinel against the backdrop of the majestic Himalayas. Swirling mist gracefully descended from the mountains, cloaking the landscape, and gently veiling the temple's grand steps that led to its entrance.

Through the dense mist, Geeta's unconscious form materialized, seemingly defying the laws of gravity. It was as though an unseen force carried her aloft, her arms hanging at her sides, and her silky hair drifting weightlessly in the breeze. The very air cradled her, guiding her toward the temple steps with a delicate devotion. Once again, her appearance was nothing short of astonishing, reminiscent of her emergence from the holy river where she narrowly escaped drowning.

Despite the harrowing ordeal of the car accident just hours before, her body appeared untouched by the calamity that had befallen her. The bruises and bloodstains had vanished, as if they were figments of a distant dream. Mud and dirt no longer marred her skin; instead, she bore an air of immaculate purity, wrapped in a white simple cotton saree of magnificent beauty.

Her suspended form glided silently through the mist of the forest, eventually coming to rest on the cold stone steps of the temple.

The surrounding atmosphere crackled with anticipation, as if the very air held its breath, awaiting the awakening of a long - dormant power.

Geeta's clenched fist tightened around the ring, her knuckles turning white. A surge of determination coursed through her veins as she stroked the stone step with a resounding thud. In that moment, her eyes snapped opened, revealing a flicker of distant knowledge and purpose. The sweet notes of a hauntingly beautiful song escaped her lips, carrying through the mist-laden air like an enchanting siren's call.

The world around her quivered, caught between the realms of dreams and reality, as Geeta's voice intertwined with the enigmatic surroundings. The temple, a silent witness to the unfolding enigma, seemed to pulse with a newfound energy, secrets waiting to be unveiled at the break of dawn.

Her Devine voice reached the balcony of the room where Talib and Dex were sleeping.

***

Perhaps it was the resonance of Geeta's prayer that stirred Talib, infusing him with a sense of renewal, while Dex remained peacefully asleep in the adjacent bed. Despite having heard the enchanting melodies of mermaids and the serenades of sirens, this was a voice unlike any other. As if a force, beyond his control, was compelling him to seek out its source. He left the room, followed the sound.

He followed the ethereal melody, until he found himself standing before a young girl, her head bowed in devotion, lost in her prayers to the god she fervently sought.

Geeta, standing outside the temple singing her morning prayer:

"Satyam, Shivam, Sundaram ..."

Talib approached Geeta. A beam of light emerged from Talib's eye and focused on Geeta. It cast a holographic screen's image in front of Talib, and displays Geeta's profile, only visible to Talib.

The holographic display presented the following information:

Name: Geeta

Age: 19 Earth Years

Mother: Pushpa

Father: Unknown

Additional Details: Geeta resides in the Temple's orphanage, belonging to the marginalized and often discriminated against Dalit caste.

Skills:

**Proficient in Archery*

**Accomplished in Judo*

**Adept at Tae Kwon Do*

**Skillful Dancer*

**Highly Trained Vocalist*

**Sprint Runner*

The holographic display vanished shortly after, leaving Talib with the newfound knowledge.

Geeta's voice had mesmerized Talib. Her hymn had the power to stir his soul and awaken emotions that he had never known existed. He stood there, transfixed by her voice and the beauty of the dawn she had summoned. Talib was witnessing his first sunrise on Earth, hearing the first time a dawn to sing.

As Geeta finished her prayer and lifted her head, she found a familiar stranger standing silently in front of her, one of the enigmatic hippie saviors.

Their eyes met once again, creating an unbreakable bond; time seemed to stand still. It was as if the stars themselves had aligned, and the universe had conspired to bring them together. Talib felt a deep connection to Geeta, a feeling that transcended the boundaries of caste and class. The son of a god rendered helpless before of low caste mortal.

Talib knew that his mission on earth was not just to find Angahrie and other sources of evil sent by Lord Iblyse, but to observe, learn and understand the beauty and complexity of human emotions, too.

As he looked into Geeta's mesmerizing eyes, he realized that he had much to learn, and that she was the key to unlocking the secrets of humanity.

For a while, she seemed to have turned into the stone and

almost as the soul trapped into her body had liberated and lifted in the clouds, and she did not remember breathing, and then a jolt of lighting revived.

She exhaled, blinked, and rose to her feet. She sprinted away, akin to a wild deer evading a pursuer.

Geeta hadn't interacted much with those beyond her village; the company of strangers made her uneasy.

Talib followed her.

As Talib was standing in front of Geeta, another son of a god, Dex, was also awaken and standing in the balcony, and watching Geeta and Talib from distance. Dex was experiencing exactly what Talib was going through: Falling in Love with Geeta.

***

As Talib chased after Geeta, his movements seemingly defying gravity, gliding as though over water. He called out, "Wait! I need to talk to you."

A gust of wind seemed to surge behind Geeta, propelling her forward like a sailboat catching the wind. She used to believe no one could outpace her, not even wild deer, but it appeared she had finally met her match.

Occasionally, Talib would vanish, only to reemerge right before her. He would pause briefly, granting her the opportunity to surge forward once more. It began to seem as though they were running for the sheer joy of running, rather than attempting to outpace one another.

Suddenly, Talib vanished. Geeta kept sprinting, occasionally glancing over her shoulder to check if Talib was trailing her. In one such look back, her frantic sprint ended abruptly as she collided head-on with Talib, who stood directly in her path.

The collision sent Geeta's world into a disorienting spin, and she began to lose consciousness. In the nick of time, Talib reacted with swift precision, reaching out to catch her in his arms with a protective embrace, and she passed out in his arms.

7

Prisoner

Opening her eyes, Geeta found herself lying in Talib's arms. He returned her gaze and the world seemed to melt away.

She did not have any feeling of uneasiness or unfamiliarity; it was as if they had known each other since the beginning of time.

And he proved her feelings were correct when she asked, "Who are you?"

"I am Talib, Geeta."

She did not even question how he knew her name as if he were supposed to. She nodded, and he released her from the fortress of his arms. Without saying a word, she rose and began walking back towards the temple. Talib watched her, smiling.

Geeta encountered the other hippie savior, looking hopelessly lost and sad, with some kind of grin on his face, as if trying to hide pain. He approached Talib, his best friend, whose happiness meant more than anything in this world, including his newly blossoming love for Geeta. Dex was ready and willing to make any sacrifice for his friendship with Talib.

As Dex neared his friend, Talib rose.

"Dex, my dear, dear friend, do you believe in love at first sight?"

Dex tried to conceal the pain on his face behind a grin, fully cognizant that his best friend had already initiated his efforts to win over Geeta. He replied, "I believe in losing your mind over a single melody."

They share a brief laugh before Dex's gaze shifted towards Geeta's figure disappearing into the morning sunlight, a pang of longing tugging at his heartstrings.

***

After having the strange encounter with Talib and Dex, Geeta walked down the village streets when she heard cries coming from a little boy. She hurried towards the commotion and found another young Dalit orphan boy named Rishi, being beaten with a stick by Mossi, a stern female attendant in her mid-50s.

"Mossi, what's wrong?" Geeta inquired. "Why are you beating him? What did he do?"

"He drank water from the mug reserved for the higher-class kids. He needs to learn his place."

Geeta pleaded, "Let go, Mossi. It was just a mistake. It won't happen again."

Mossi pushed Rishi away, he fell on the ground, sobbing. Mossi's anger did not diminish.

"I wish you and your kind never existed!"

"Well," Geeta began, "that would be a big problem, Mossi. Your toilets won't get cleaned, and the whole village will stink."

Geeta winked at Rishi, trying to comfort him, but Mossi's hostility remained.

"Just die and go to hell!"

"We don't need to die, Mossi. We're already in hell!"

Geeta took Rishi by his arm and led him away, wiping his tears.

Mossi threatened to complain to Bapu.

"Ever since Bapu assigned you as the morning prayer singer, you think you're the same as us!"

As they walked away, Geeta leaned into Rishi and whispered, "Don't worry, one day this will come to an end, and there will be no more separate mugs for the people in the village to drink water, regardless of who they may be."

"Seriously?"

Geeta nodded.

"I promise," Geeta assured him. "A day will come when we all live in this world equally."

"Are You going to do it?"

Geeta nodded, again.

"How?" asked Rishi.

"With the help of gods."

As Rishi found reassurance, Geeta and the boy walked away, leaving Mossi behind, still rambling more threats and curses in her native tongue.

Rishi saw his friends calling him to join them in the play. He freed himself from Geeta's grip and dashed to join his friends, leaving Geeta alone.

***

As she started to walk home, a heavy weight of exhaustion and disbelief tugged at her steps. The world felt like a different place after the surreal events she had witnessed and experienced since yesterday. Her thoughts were a tumultuous storm, each thundering heartbeat echoing the chaos in her mind.

Suddenly, a police car materialized on the road ahead, its ominous presence like a precursor of an impending tempest. The vehicle came to an abrupt stop before Geeta, the screech of tires punctuating the gravity of the situation. From the car emerged a middle-aged police officer, Inspector Sameer Khan, his countenance stern.

Geeta's heart raced, her breath catching in her throat as her eyes locked onto the officer. His question hung in the air, a fateful inquiry that would shatter the fragile semblance of reality she clung to.

"Are you Geeta?" he demanded, his voice a heavy thud in the stillness.

Her brows furrowed in confusion, she could only manage a bewildered nod in response, her voice momentarily lost amidst the whirlwind of emotions raging within her.

As the officer retrieved a pair of handcuffs, the world around Geeta seemed to blur. His words struck with a force that left her reeling, like a punch to the gut, as he laid out the charges, "You are under arrest for stealing Thakur Roy's car, damaging it, and causing the death of Asha Dewal."

The weight of his accusations crashed down upon her, an avalanche of disbelief and horror threatening to consume her.

Her heart shattered at the mention of Asha's name, her

friend's untimely demise an unimaginable nightmare. The realization was a violent shockwave that tore through her soul.

"No, no, this can't be true," Geeta cried out, her voice cracking with the weight of her denial. "I didn't do anything!"

But her desperate pleas fell on deaf ears, the officer's determination unyielding. The metallic clink of handcuffs closed around her wrists, their cold touch a cruel reminder of the reality she was trapped in. He dragged her toward the police jeep, her resistance futile against the inexorable pull of authority. As she was being escorted away, her eyes scanned the growing crowd, which had assembled like looming storm clouds to witness her plight. Among the onlookers stood Asha's parents, their tearful eyes mirroring the tragedy that had descended upon their lives.

Geeta's heart weighed heavily as her gaze met theirs, her own eyes brimming with a blend of sorrow and helplessness. She couldn't help but notice the looming figures of Thakur Roy and his gang members positioned ominously behind the distraught parents.

The jeep's engine roared to life, its thunderous growl overpowering the surrounding gasps and hushed whispers.

As the vehicle bore her away, Geeta's unwavering gaze clung to a handful of mournful faces in the crowd. The burden of their accusing stares, combined with the crushing grief of losing her friend, left her with a profound sense of isolation and abandonment—a solitary figure branded by the unrelenting hand of destiny.

$$8$$

Proposal

Within the dimly lit walls of a cramped local police station, Geeta found herself seated across from Inspector Sameer Khan. She looked exhausted; his interrogation had been relentless.

The room exuded a musty atmosphere. Harsh fluorescent lights cast a stark glare over the worn furniture and faded paint, giving the setting an air of both discomfort and unease.

Inspector Khan, a stern figure known for his commitment to the law, commanded the room's attention. His weary eyes held a glimpse of the challenges he faced, navigating the delicate balance between enforcing justice and battling the grip of corruption that sometimes tainted his higher-ups.

Geeta's frustration and distress were obvious; her trembling hands cradled her head, and the echoes of her sobs reverberated in the air. With a mixture of exasperation and determination, she tried to convey her innocence to Inspector Khan, desperation coloring her words,

"Please sir, you have to believe me. We took a rickshaw from Shanti to Freak Street, not Thakur's car. After the movie, we were drugged and forced into that car. That's all I remember. Why won't you talk to Abdul, the rickshaw driver?"

"We've already spoken to Abdul," Inspector Khan replied with a sigh. "He claims no recollection of driving you and Asha to the movie theater."

Geeta's head shook in disbelief, the injustice of it all pressing upon her. Amid the tense atmosphere, a constable discreetly approached Inspector Khan, whispering a message that prompted the officer to jot down hurried notes. He didn't raise his gaze or make eye contact as he spoke, his words bearing both finality and release. "Very well. You are free to go. Your lawyer has secured your bail."

He indicated a figure standing near the doorway, a man whose presence seemed to materialize at that moment.

"Keep us informed of your whereabouts."

Geeta's head swam. The man before her wore the attire of a lawyer. A warm smile accompanied his turn, revealing his true identity as her savior: Talib.

***

Geeta and Talib stepped into a rickshaw outside the police station. The ride back to Shanti was not without its moments of awkwardness, Geeta finding herself in close proximity to a man for the first time in her life. Growing up she had enjoyed her loneliness, and the only companionship she did forge was with Asha. The rickshaw's occasional sways to avoid potholes or weaving through pedestrians brought them closer together, a subtle dance of gravity or, perhaps, intents of

Talib. Throughout it all, occasionally wiping her tears, Geeta maintained her silence, her gaze fixed on the passing scenery beyond, as if the landscape held answers to the questions stirring within her.

As they neared the village, Geeta's voice emerged, a soft whisper laden with sorrow.

"What do you want from me?"

"Nothing, actually. Well, perhaps your help."

He sensed the unspoken question in her eyes, the curiosity of how a Dalit girl could provide aid to someone of his background.

"See, I am writing a book about inequalities among people of Shanti and the unjust society it has built. I was hoping you could help me understand how it works, or perhaps help me to come up with some solutions for this unfair treatment among the people."

In that moment, Geeta felt a glimmer of empathy emanating from him, a recognition of shared humanity transcending social divides. Turning her gaze away once more, she fought to contain the storm of emotions welling within her, masking the tears that threatened to spill.

Silence enveloped them once again, the weight of unspoken words hanging in the air.

Finally, Geeta's voice broke through, laden with grief, "Asha was a good girl. She didn't deserve to die so young. She was my best friend, my only friend."

Tears began to trace paths down her cheeks, like monsoon rain.

Talib felt her pain.

"Listen, in two days we are going on a trip to climb the

Himalayas; I think, it would be great if you could also come. It would help you to cope with your loss and other things that are going on."

The offer hung in the air, a potential balm for Geeta's wounded soul. Gathering her strength, she took a deep breath, using the edge of her sari to wipe away her tears.

"I need to ask Bapu, first."

The rickshaw entered the village of Shanti.

9

Climb

Bapu had given Geeta permission to join the excursion without any hesitation. Perhaps, he thought it would be better for Geeta and the village if she would go away from Shanti for some time: the quiet and monotonous village of Shanti was having difficulties coping with these series of unusual events.

The small group of climbers embarked on their journey towards Langtang Lirung Summit, comparatively shorter than the other surrounding peaks of Himalayas. Initially, Geeta's heart was heavy with the weight of Asha's absence, but it started to become lighter as they gained altitude. The path ahead was a mixture of treacherous terrain and breathtaking beauty.

On the first day of their journey, they climb for the whole day, the enigmatic mountaineers decided to take a break. The Sherpa and his team had pitched the tents, tied the yaks and dzos, and had cooked the dinner.

Climbing those summits perhaps was not a big task for Dex and Talib, but what was surprising was that Geeta was keeping up with them shoulder to shoulder.

So, when the trio sat by the campfire. Talib and Dex next to each other, and Geeta opposite, Talib could not help to not compliment Geeta.

"Looks like you have climbed these mountains several times before."

She smiled shyly and nodded nervously, as she stared blankly at ember sparks flying from the firepit. Then, remembering what Talib actually want to hear from her during the climb, she kept her head down, without making an eye contact, she began, "I don't know when the people came to live in these majestic regions, but we were just simple mountain people, and the Shanti was a peaceful village.

"Legend tells us that one day she came down from the peaks of the Poon Hills," she pointed towards a distant summit, "And went inside the temple up there; nobody knows what happened inside that temple, but later the high priest came out and he had a new sermon for us, how to live our lives based on the new caste systems.

"Nobody saw her after that; some say she became the soul of the high priest."

"Who was she?" Dex asked.

"Angahrie, the black goddess." She looked towards the Poon Hill again, "We will pass her temple, near that peak."

Dex and Talib looked at each other—at last, a clue about whereabouts of Angahrie.

***

The next day of their ascent, Talib walked alongside

Geeta, the crunch of his footsteps marking the rhythm of her heartbeat.

Geeta found herself opening up about the caste system, the scars it left on the society, and the countless struggles she had witnessed: abductions, murders, and other hideous acts.

She shared folk tales of the village's early days of their religion, the teachings of compassion and peace that have shaped their community. Talib absorbed her stories intently.

As the days passed and the altitude grew, so did the bond between Geeta and Talib. With every shared step and whispered conversation, they discovered common ground amidst their differences. With each passing day, Geeta felt a growing sense of strength within herself.

As they neared the final base camp of the Summit, the towering summit of Langtang Lirung felt both exhilarating and humbling. The journey had been a mix of physical exertion and profound introspection. As they climbed higher and higher, Geeta gained more and more confidence in herself; she had gained a new perspective on her own life and her role in the world. Now when she would talk, she looked directly into one's eye, kept her head high, and walked tall.

***

On the night before they reached the summit, under the starlit canvas of the Himalayan night, the campfire crackled, casting dancing shadows on the faces of the weary climbers. The chilly air was made warmer by the camaraderie that had developed among them. As they huddled around the fire, Dex leaned forward, his eyes fixed on Geeta.

"Geeta," he began, "What does an ideal world look like to you?"

Geeta's gaze shifted from the mesmerizing flames to Dex's earnest expression. They had shared glances, nods, and smiles, but this was the first time Dex had directly asked the question, sitting next to her, while Talib was sitting on the other side.

She was at first a little surprised and shy to be directly addressed by Dex, then she took a moment to ponder the question, her thoughts traveling through the intricacies of her experiences.

"An ideal world for me would be the one where everyone is treated equally, with dignity and fairness. It wouldn't matter the color of their skin, their race, or even their gender. Where children do not get to eat or receive education based on their caste"

Talib, seated nearby, nodded in agreement, his eyes reflecting the flames.

"In this world," she continued, "no one would be held back by their caste or social status. No one would be denied opportunities because of their place of birth or origin of their ancestors.

"People would be free to chase their dreams without being shackled by outdated norms. They all should be able to enter the temple to worship their gods."

Dex's brows furrowed as he absorbed her words, his eyes showing genuine interest.

"But do you think such a world is possible? The caste system, the inequalities... they seem deeply ingrained."

Geeta's gaze remained steady and her determination unwavering.

"I believe it's possible. Change starts with awareness, with conversations like the ones we're having right now. If we can challenge the status quo and inspire others to do the same, we can create ripples of change that spread far and wide."

"And how old are you?" Talib asked. "And where did you learn to speak like that?"

Geeta smiled shyly, "Sneaking into those classrooms at night reserved for the higher caste students was not easy."

They all chuckled.

Dex inhaled. "Your perspective on a just world for everyone resonates deeply with me. Perhaps the gods have chosen not to intervene because they desire us to transcend them, to demonstrate that unity and compassion hold greater power than any man-made divisions."

Talib yawned.

"On that uplifting note, shall we call it a night? We'll need to rise early to complete the final leg of our journey."

Although in reality, both Dex and Talib were eager to explore Angahrie's Lair, Dex pretended to be especially excited about reaching the heights of Mount Everest.

"I can hardly contain my anticipation for the breathtaking view from the top of the world tomorrow! And if had some spare time, we could go and visit the Temple of Angahrie, too," he said, looking at Talib. "Right?"

Talib played along, "Of course … Of course."

Geeta smiled knowingly; this was familiar territory for her. She had ascended these peaks numerous times and uncovered some of the mountains' hidden secrets that remained unknown to others.

10

Lair of the Beast

The next day dawned with the first light barely gracing the horizon. In a hurry, they devoured a quick breakfast before embarking on the final leg of their ascent.

The unforgiving conditions tested their mettle at every step. Thin air made each breath a struggle, the howling wind mercilessly stung their faces, and the ice beneath their boots threatened to give way at any moment. Battling through the biting cold, they pressed on, determined to conquer both the mountain and the lurking darkness that awaited them.

As they navigated the treacherous terrain, a sudden gust of wind carried away the echoes of a distant avalanche, a reminder of the perilous nature of their quest. The elements seemed to conspire against them, and in a heart-wrenching moment, one of their donkeys succumbed to the harsh conditions, leaving a somber trail of loss amid the relentless climb.

The grueling hike lasted half a day, and as they neared the pinnacle, the imposing lair of Angahrie emerged ominously on the horizon. The Sherpas, seasoned climbers with stoic expressions, couldn't conceal an undercurrent of fear that was evident in their eyes—a sentiment that mirrored the apprehension in Geeta's gaze.

The temple appeared deserted, as if untouched by human presence for centuries. An unsettling unease settled upon the crew, prompting Talib to make a commanding decision, "Dex and I will venture inside alone. The rest of you, wait here."

Geeta and the crew remained at a cautious distance as Talib and Dex approached the temple entrance, which a colossal skull carved into the granite heart of the Himalayas.

***

Within the temple's oppressive darkness, cobwebs clung to the corners, and a legion of cockroaches scurried away from the invaders' flashlight beams. As they ventured deeper, sinister shadows danced upon the walls, telling tales of centuries-old horrors. A noxious, pungent odor enveloped the temple, while a few prayer bells hung ominously silent.

Their search yielded little, and they returned to the waiting crew.

As they continued their journey, faint, haunting echoes of temple bells resonated from within the forsaken shrine.

***

Upon finally reaching the summit of the majestic Himalayas, Talib, Geeta, and Dex were overcome with awe, although each of them has visited sites like this many times before. The view before them was nothing short of miraculous. Towering peaks, adorned with glistening snow crowns, seemed to reach for the very heavens. Vast expanses of untamed wilderness whispered the secrets of the universe to their souls.

"I bet you never have reached such a height before, right?" Geeta said, her excitement bubbling.

Talib and Dex nodded, trying to hide their smirks.

Talib's gaze followed the highest peak of the Himalayas, Everest, where G.F.I.T. had landed a few days ago, concealed in the lingering clouds that was not able reach the summit.

11

Charmed

They camped for a single night at the summit, then began their descent the following day. After having an early supper, Talib, seated beneath the shade of a towering Himalayan tree, letting his fingers dance upon a yellow pad emitting a faint, otherworldly glow, an advanced communication device for Devine beings.

From his side satchel, which also concealed his sword, he withdrew a pen and a tablet like devices, and began to meticulously document his thoughts and revelations since arriving on Earth.

Day 21, he began his journal entry.

My pursuit of Angahrie persists, though the trail remains elusive. Our suspicions regarding Lord Iblyse's influence over human minds appear substantiated. The caste system bears signs of manipulation, and the fragility of humanity deeply concerns me.

Talib paused, reflecting on the rapid advancement of humans.

Humanity has made significant strides since the dawn of agriculture, erecting monumental structures, harnessing advanced technologies, and delving into the mysteries of the universe through physics and chemistry. It is as though they have been entrusted with divine knowledge prematurely, challenging even the gods. However, they have yet to invent the Internet and social media, still in the early days of computer technologies, specially, AI and Quantum Computing.

His pen wavered as he considered something profoundly personal, and he bit his lip in contemplation. Then, he added a personal note.

I have encountered an extraordinary human named Geeta. Despite her low caste, her spirit and character are unparalleled. I understand the complexities this introduces, but I cannot deny my feelings. She aids me in comprehending the intricacies of human emotions and sentiments. Father, if you read this, I hope you can find it in your heart to understand.

Talib's hand trembled as he concluded his entry, his gaze fixed upon the pad, a whirlwind of emotions surging within him. With a deep breath, he pressed the send button at the corner of the pad, transmitting the log to the League of Gods.

The yellow writing pad chimed softly, confirming the successful transmission. Talib looked up, his eyes meeting Geeta's as she approached him, her presence stirring a tempest of emotions within his heart.

***

In the heart of Kai-Nat, Lord Shakta stood within a bustling command center, a realm of holographic screens that painted an intricate tapestry of charts, graphs, and data. Skilled technicians, their attire sleek and precise, moved with a fluidity that matched the rhythm of the machines they manipulated, their holographic keyboards dancing with light and information.

Amidst this intricate web of technology, as the text rolled on the display, Lord Shakta's demeanor remained inscrutable, a mask that hardly betrayed his inner thoughts. His piercing gaze scanned through a sea of incoming texts, and as he stumbled upon the name "Geeta," an unmistakable shadow crossed his features. Whether the named *Geeta* or mentioned of *Dalit* caused him displeasure was not evident.

"Roll back!" His command sliced through the ambient hum of activity.

The assistant swiftly complied, magnifying the text on Lord Shakta's screen.

Lord Shakta, directed, "Stop!"

Standing next to him, Lady Mohobut, mother of Lady Khoob-Sue-Rut, clenched his hand.

Lady Mohobut who had been one of many companions of Lord Shakta for years, had some high hopes for her daughter marrying Talib one day. She had expressed her desire on numerous occasions to Lord Shakta, who seemed to be in favour of it, too. But now, the content of the message from Planet Earth seemed to be ruining all her plans.

The lord and the lady read the words again, as if trying to confirm that they were indeed real. Lady Mohobut brought her face to touch Lord Shakta's arm.

"This will ruin my daughter's future. Who will marry my poor daughter now?"

Lord Shakta not paying any attention to her crying, seemed lost in his own world, "The prophecy."

He snaps out of his momentary reverie and responds to Lady Mohobut, his concerns evident.

"Right now, I am more concerned about the prophecy being fulfilled."

"What prophecy?"

Ignoring her question, Lord Shakta contemplated the implications of what he had read. He then turned to another assistant with a decisive tone, "Compose a response to Talib, as follows..."

The assistant's fingers danced across the holographic keyboard, crafting a message that would soon find its way to Talib's tablet.

****

As Talib, still seated beneath the towering Himalayan tree, received the incoming message from his father, the contents of the text appeared far from what he had anticipated. His visage drained of color, a hint of moisture welled up in his eyes, quickly brushed aside with a trembling hand.

Dex, who had approached Talib, noticed the profound shift in his friend's countenance. "You look as if you have seen death. What's wrong?"

Talib wordlessly handed him the yellow pad, his expression a complex interplay of emotions. Dex took a deep breath and began to read aloud, his voice carrying the weight of the message, "It seems you've lost sight of your mission's purpose.

"I am issuing a direct order for both you and Dex to return home immediately. There are matters of utmost importance that require your attention here. The G.I.F.T. has been programmed to depart from Earth precisely at midnight, 12 AM. Ensure you both are on board."

Dex glanced at Geeta, her silhouette a distant figure, feeding the birds while perched upon a solitary rock. He then shifted his gaze back to Talib, who took the communication device out of Dex's hand, put it his satchel along his sword, started marching forward towards Geeta, with an unwavering determination in his stride. Then, he turned to Dex, while kept walking. "Let the Sherpas know that we won't be needing them any longer, they can return to the village.

"I am not leaving this planet without her," with a defiance in his voice, he announced.

As Talib drew nearer to Geeta, a radiant smile spread across her face. Her eyes sparkled with delight, and she beckoned him to join her with an eager hand gesture. Talib leaped up onto the rock where she stood, his curiosity piqued. Geeta extended her arm, directing his gaze toward a monumental cliff that dominated the landscape.

"Do you see that?" she inquired.

Talib squinted, following her finger. His eyes widened in awe. There it was – a colossal, fossilized T-Rex, ensconced within the very heart of an immense boulder nestled in the Himalayan valley.

With a sense of wonder and reverence, Geeta ran towards the newly unveiled fossil. Tabil followed her.

The fossil might have remained hidden for millions of years, a silent witness to the ever-changing Earth. Shifts in climate due to global warming, however, had unveiled this ancient relic, a stark reminder of the planet's tumultuous history.

As they drew closer to their discovery, Geeta couldn't contain the childhood dream she had nurtured for so long. She whispered it to Talib, her voice a soft echo against the valley's grandeur.

"I used to fantasize of riding a giant majestic creature, like this." Her fingers delicately traced the contours of the creature's enormous mouth etched in bolder, bridging the gap between reality and her cherished imagination.

"I wished it was alive," she said, "and I could ride it like a dragon in fairy tales."

For a moment, Talib forgot the bad news he had received earlier and couldn't help but smile at her childlike wonder, his fingers brushing the fossilized tail. Unexpectedly, it shifted slightly. He winked at the T-Rex, and the enormous eye blinked back at him.

The resurrection of this ancient beast began slowly, unnoticed by Geeta.

"This may not be the right time to tell you all this, but I have no choice, and you have to believe what I say," he began.

She tilted her head in curiosity and allowed Talib to lead her to clearing.

"Geeta, I'm not who you think I am," he said, before pausing. "I am a son of a god."

She burst into laughter in disbelief, gesturing toward the fossil.

"Sure, and this is my pet," she teased.

"Well, he is now."

T-Rex had been charmed and Geeta was about to. Before she could react, Talib suddenly lifted her off the ground and started running, then began to soar through the air, carrying her in his arms.

At first, her screams mixed with delight and fear echoed in the valley, but once she realized that they were flying over the valley, her screams got trapped inside her opened mouth and her eyes widened in panic, as Talib was no longer running on the ground; he was flying. Then, the thrill became too much for Geeta, and she passed out in his arms, once again.

It seemed he was flying towards the full moon carrying her in his arms. In the distance, on the highest peak of the Himalayas, G.I.F.T. was waiting. As he cradled her, Talib gently descended to the ground and walked toward the spacecraft, G.I.F.T.

***

Inside, one of the monitors displayed the remaining take off time:

Time to Take Off Remaining:

35.00

34.59

33.58

12

Prophecy

Geeta regained consciousness soon after Talib carried her into the spacecraft. Her world shifted between wonder and confusion. Emotions threatened to drown her. Her senses were overwhelmed by the blinking lights, monitors, and computers that surrounded her, each one a testament to a world beyond her wildest dreams.

Talib's presence and his cautious yet caring words provided her with some anchor amid this sea of technology.

"Look, perhaps all of this appears like magic to you, but these are called scientific advancements and technology that, well, you humans will be able to achieve in the future, too."

Geeta had seen a few sci-fi movies but never thought that this could exist beyond fantasies.

Talib moved closer to her. His trembling hand found hers, a touch filled with emotion that words could not convey.

"I..." Talib began.

Geeta locked her gaze on his, feeling the significance

of this moment hanging in the air, a connection that transcended explanation.

"It's just happening... I... we must leave Earth within the next half-hour...", Talib struggled to find the right words. "... And I just cannot leave without you." He hesitated, his voice catching with emotion as he continued, "Will you come with me?"

At that moment she fully realized that she could not live on Earth without him beside her.

The spacecraft jolted as if struck by a meteor. Talib and Geeta lost their balance as chaos erupted around them. The pounding door was deafening.

The countdown for liftoff continued relentlessly:

20.00

19.59

19.58

***

Meanwhile, back at the campsite, Dex frantically searched for the Sherpas but found nothing but scattered belongings, and some splattered blood streaks, as they were mutilated and dragged out by some beast. Faint ringing sounds echoed through the air, drawing him closer to the temple of Angahrie. The oil lamps were lit, and mutilated bodies of the sherpas lay in a gruesome pile at the altar. The beast had awakened.

***

A sheer force tore open G.I.F.T.'s metal doors. They opened halfway, revealing Angahrie, her eyes ablaze with rage. She stormed into the spacecraft.

The prophecy from 4000 years ago was reverberating in her ears, as the old hideous witch revealed it.

"Be aware of the day the prophecy will come true. The day a son of a god will fall in love with a low-caste Dalit girl and make love to her.

"That day, your powers will be gone, your spells will be reverted, and you will return to your original form: a slimy reptile without any powers or magic, living the rest of your life in the swamp." The witch's vial giggles rang in Angahrie's ears.

The fear that had engulfed Angahrie since her incarnation was about to come true. She was not going to let the prophecy be fulfilled at any cost.

As Angahrie marched towards Talib and Geeta, his hand moved instinctively to pull out his sword from his shoulder bag, but Angahrie raised her hand, turning him into a stone statue.

A thunderous crack of lightning and heavy rain ensued.

Angahrie's venomous gaze locked onto Geeta, and she seized her by the throat, lifting her effortlessly.

"You low-caste, bastard, bitch!"

Angahrie hissed, her fangs dripping venom. She punctured Geeta's arm, poison coursing through Geeta's veins, before she was thrown outside the spacecraft.

Once again, Geeta's anguished cry filled the air as she landed in the mud, her arm turning a sickly purple from the venom.

***

With his satchel on his back, katana inside, Dex, perched on a cliff, heard Geeta's distant scream piercing through the night. With determination, Dex leaped from the cliff, soaring toward the source of Geeta's distress.

The full moon disappeared behind the clouds. Thunder rumbled, lighting flashed, and rain continued to pour as Dex floated in air through the eerie blackness, determined to reach Geeta.

***

As the storm raged on outside, monitors blinked to life inside the craft, and the countdown to departure continued. The vessel, seemingly ready for liftoff, awaited the command of its masters.

Angahrie began her transformation into a python. She approached Talib, now a beautiful marble statue, her mouth widening to an unnatural size as she began to swallow him whole.

Geeta, barely conscious, watched this horror unfold from outside. Her mouth opened to scream, but no sound came out.

Angahrie's pack of snakes, the Chingahries, closed in on Geeta, ready to strike their prey.

With great effort and pain, she rose from the ground, her body soaked in mud and rain. Adrenaline propelled her into a frenzied sprint, her heart pounding with fear.

She tripped over a branch. Before she could get to her feet, a python loomed, its fangs dripping with venom, poised to strike.

Suddenly, a mighty katana sliced through the air, severing the snake's head in a single, swift motion.

Dex's eyes blazed with determination as green blood dripped from his katana's gleaming blade. His hair altered between different shades, making it hard to pinpoint just one emotion.

He knelt and held Geeta into his arms, and asked, "Where is Talib?"

"He's gone!" She pointed towards the G.I.F.T. "That witch killed him and devoured him whole."

"No, she can't kill him; he is a son of a god, he is immortal. He is only under her spell, and we need to free him."

Dex set Geeta back on the ground and took off towards the approaching nest of snakes, the Chingahries, slicing through them like stalks of wheat.

Geeta's anguished screams once again echoed through the air.

Angahrie loomed menacingly over her. Geeta's body writhed helplessly, etching desperate tracks into the ground as Angahrie's relentless jaws threatened to consume her.

***

Inside the spacecraft, the monitor was displaying the remaining time:

01.44

01.33

01.32

***

Outside the spacecraft, Dex's eyes bore into the nightmarish scene before him. Laser-like rays emitted from his brown eyes, displaying a holographic screen, rapidly calculating the dire situation. Less than two minutes remained before the G.I.F.T. would take off.

Angahrie's grip tightened around Geeta's trembling feet, relentlessly pulling her deeper into the abyss of her maw.

The holographic screen, a communication device, was relaying instructions from the command center of League of Gods, Planet Kai-Nat. The screen pulsed with urgency to calculate the current situation and it revealed the sole viable solution. The words on the screen delivered the grim verdict:

Your current powers are no match for Angahrie's. You must free Geeta and get on G.I.F.T. to leave Planet Earth immediately. No time left. The only viable solution is...

Anguish contorted Dex's face as he read the remainder of the text. His teeth clenched, the weight of the moment pressing heavily upon him. With unwavering determination, he had made his mind.

00.55

00.54

00.53

***

Dex's grip on his katana tightened as he lunged towards the monstrous python. In a blur of motion, his blade sliced through Geeta's feet, freeing her from Angahrie's relentless grip.

Dex's heart bore the immense burden of his choice, but he knew it was the sole means to rescue Geeta from impending doom: to halt the venom's advance within her body and get on the spacecraft before it would take off, he had to sever her legs just below the ankle. The color of his hair turned midnight blue.

Out of the dense forest, the resurrected T-Rex, brought back to life by Talib, emerged with a sudden and thunderous presence. With a ferocious roar that echoed through the jungle, it revealed its formidable array of teeth. Trying to ward off the menace its master faced, this massive creature instinctively positioned itself protectively between Geeta and Angahrie and the encroaching snakes.

00:10

00:09

00:08

***

Dex scooped Geeta into his arms, rain cascading like tears down his face as he dashed towards the awaiting spacecraft. Geeta's body was a canvas of wounds– one arm hung limp as if shattered. Her legs bore deep gashes below the knees. Blood gushed below her ankles from the wounds where her feet used to be. Dex movements were as fast as light, trying to beat the clock.

00:03

00:02

00:01

As soon as Dex entered the spacecraft, the doors sealed shut with a bang behind him.

00:00

With a surge of power, the vessel launched into space, taking Geeta light years away from Earth.

***

In the distance, Angahrie and her Chingahries engaged in a fierce battle with the T-Rex, the brave loyal beast providing a chance for them to escape.

The T-Rex fought ferociously, displaying its terrifying

teeth, determined to prevent Angahrie and her minions from reaching G.I.F.T.

***

Inside G.I.F.T., in her fleeting moments of consciousness, Geeta's thoughts were a singular echo: Talib.

The name reverberated through the chaos, a lifeline in the storm of agony that enveloped her.

Growing up at the orphanage, she had always dreamed that one day a Rajkumar, a prince charming, would come, and take her away, beyond this village and its segregated system and caste-based ways of life.

But not even her worst nightmares, Geeta had ever imagined that a son of a god would descend on earth and fall in love with her. Then, she had to leave earth, half-dead, without him!

Amidst the tumult of pain and uncertainty, Geeta's resolve crystallized. A fire kindled within her, an unshakable determination. She promised to herself before she drifted away:

No matter what sacrifices I have to make, one day I will return to free my love and reclaim it. I will shatter the shackles of societal bias and free my people in Shati to live in just and fair world.

Little did she know that she would end up creating this world of her dreams on an exoplanet for the last of humanity to save them from becoming extinct.

This Dalit girl, who was once not even allowed to enter the temple where gods were worshiped, was about to prove to the universe that she was worthy of not only loving a son of a god, but also becoming a goddess herself: A Devi.

The journey had just begun.

13

Part Human Part Machine

Inside the spacecraft's Dex sprinted toward the doors adorned with the inscription *Medical Lab.* The lab was equipped with highly advanced technologies to analyze a patient's condition and recommend and perform needed medical procedures.

Dex laid Geeta on a marble slab, her clothing blood-soaked and mud-caked. Her arm, bitten by Angahrie, had turned purple.

As Dex removed her torn clothing. He gazed at the holographic displays for instructions on what to do next.

Dex lifted Geeta off the slab and submerged her whole body below the neck in a liquid-filled glass container. Held in place by hydraulics, Geeta's body froze and turned light blue in the solution.

***

With half-opened eyes, the T-Rex lay, drawing its last breaths, while the horde of Chingahries relentlessly stabbed it with swords and knives. Angahrie, her fangs dripping with blood, stood nearby, fixating on a massive glacier. Her thirst for revenge remained unquenched; she craved to inflict more pain on those connected to Geeta than a mere dinosaur.

With a sinister grin on her face, she glanced at Sharara and remarked, "I doubt I could stomach that son of a god for too long. Anyway, I've had my fill of this cold. Let's go somewhere warm."

Angahrie started marching, rubbing her belly. Sharara and the rest of the Chingahries followed their diabolic leader. The huge glacier began to tremble, a forewarning of an impending avalanche.

***

In the silent embrace of the icy night, a sudden rumble disrupted the serene slumber of Shanti. Bapu awoke with a jolt, swiftly abandoning his bed, and rushed outside the temple. The villagers remained peacefully unaware in their collective slumber.

With each passing moment, the rumble intensified and the ground under his feet felt like jelly, making hard for Bapu to maintain his balance.

In the eerie glow of the moonlight, Bapu saw the mountainside cracked open, and an avalanche of snow and ice cascaded down with a ferocity that seemed to defy the tranquility of the night. He started to scream of impending danger.

The roar of the avalanche drowned out any attempts at warning as it swallowed the sleeping village whole.

The frozen torrent devoured homes and lives indiscriminately, the cries of the awakening villagers blending with the tumultuous noise of the avalanche.

The icy tendrils of the avalanche reached into every corner of Shanti, including the temple, and enveloped Bapu in its tempestuous force. The once-thriving community was obliterated, leaving behind a silent tableau of destruction illuminated only by the pale glow of the moon.

***

Dex stood outside the Medical Lab as he watched Geeta through the two-way mirror. The lab was devoid of any living presence, and the only sounds were the mechanical hum and the hiss of hydraulic pistons in motion. A soft blue light bathed the chamber, casting an otherworldly glow upon the scene.

A series of intricate mechanical devices and medical instruments surrounded Geeta, poised to perform the needed procedures to save her life.

The chamber was adorned with sleek holographic displays that hovered around her, projecting vital information and visual representations of each procedure.

These displays provided a glimpse into the remarkable fusion of science and technology that would empower Geeta to become a fighting machine.

Dex cast a quick glance at one of the displays beside him. A mechanical voice emanated from the monitor, "Permission needed to proceed with the required operation requested."

Gritting his teeth, Dex bit his lip and commanded, "Proceed."

The shade of his hair turned dark blue.

The eerie sound of a mechanical devices starting to pierce through the air. Tears started to roll down Dex's face, as a sound, similar to one would hear in a butcher's shop when slicing the meat, started to fill the room. The transformation of Geeta into an indestructible machine had begun.

A mechanical arm extended from the chamber walls, equipped with precision tools, delicately severing Geeta's arm above the shoulder. The hydraulic pistons provided support as her body is positioned for the procedure.

The holographic displays nearby showcased real-time images of the process. Labels and diagrams explained the benefits of the bionic limbs, highlighting enhanced strength, agility, and the ability to adapt to various environments.

Holographic displays accompanied the mechanical arms as they attached the bionic limbs. Diagrams demonstrated the sophisticated technology behind the limbs, showcasing their versatility, durability, and seamless integration with Geeta's body.

The chamber began to fill with a dense mist as hydraulic pumps engaged, releasing a specialized chemical compound. The mist enveloped Geeta's body, initiating a regenerative process. The holographic displays illustrated the regenerative properties of the mist. Schematic animations revealed how it stimulated tissue regrowth, accelerated healing, and fortified her biological systems.

Within the mist, the mechanical arms equipped with intricate mechanisms emerged from the tank. They attached bionic limbs, constructed from gleaming alloys to Geeta's severed limbs. The limbs connected seamlessly, a fusion of human and machine.

A medical device resembling a hovering orb descends from above, emitting a focused beam of light. It delicately shaved Geeta's beautiful long hair while another device collects the hair, dissolving it within the liquid surrounding her.

A mechanical apparatus resembling a robotic surgeon approached Geeta's exposed skull. It drilled into her cranium, creating a portal for the implantation of a highly advanced AI chip, capable of processing trillions of data points in a nanosecond.

The holographic display highlighted the AI chip's capabilities and benefits. It showcased an array of subjects: scientific discoveries, combat techniques, and a wealth of knowledge spanning civilizations. The holographic images demonstrated how the chip augments Geeta's intellect, granting her unprecedented access to information and combat expertise.

A complex mechanism inserted the AI chip into Geeta's brain, connecting it to her neural pathways. The chip began to emit pulsating lights, signifying its activation and integration with her consciousness.

After completing all the necessary procedures, the mechanical devices and medical instruments receded into the chamber walls.

The liquid within the tank slowly drained away as hydraulic mechanisms retract, gently lowering Geeta halfway onto a platform within the chamber. Geeta emerged from the solution tank, her unconscious body, suspended with hydraulic attachments, floating above the tank in the mid air. Part human. Part Machine.

The next day, after all the surgeries were completed, clad

in a hospital gown, Geeta was transferred to a stretcher-like bed.

Dex entered the room and leaned in close, his hand gently touching her forehead, and whispering her name.

Then, he leaned close to her face, gently moving his finger on her cheek.

There was no immediate response. Dex tried again, softly tapping her chin, whispering, "Geeta!"

Her eyelids fluttered slightly, followed by a deep breath as her eyes opened. Her gaze fixed upon Dex, trying to remember the previous chain of events that led her to this bed, and then she glanced down, taking in her new mechanical limbs: one arm and two legs.

Suddenly, without warning, her newly attached mechanical arm seized Dex by the throat. She leapt off the bed, pinning Dex against the wall with a firm grip.

Dex's face remained composed, showing only a hint of discomfort. After all, he too was a son of a god.

Geeta brought her shaven head closer to Dex's face, her voice laced with anger. "What have you done to me!"

Dex raised his free hand, attempting to explain. "This was necessary to save your life."

Tears streamed down Geeta's face. Dex paused for a moment, choosing his words carefully.

"I need to go back and free Talib from Angahrie's spell. While I'm away, I need someone capable of piloting the G.I.F.T. and helping us return to it.

"You couldn't acquire this knowledge on your own within your lifetime. Now, you possess the wisdom that humans will develop over the next few millennia. You're skilled in advanced warfare and an expert in mortal combat."

Geeta's grip on Dex loosened, releasing his neck.

She raised her human hand to touch her shaved head, slowly starting to grasp the necessary sacrifice and the greater purpose.

"I used to love my hair."

"Don't worry, it will grow back before the next time you see Talib."

A faint smile appeared on Geeta's face as she drifted into the memories of him.

Dex's demeanor relaxed upon realizing that Geeta still retained her innocence and human emotions, despite the extensive transformation she had undergone.

His expression softened as he placed his hand on her mechanical arm.

"You still have your innocent heart, Geeta. That part of you remains untouched, no matter what changes you've experienced."

Geeta's eyes met Dex's, searching for truth in his words. A flicker of hope and relief passed through her gaze as she began to accept the profound fusion of humanity and machinery that now defined her existence.

14

Nineveh

After scouring the immense expanse of the Sahara Desert for several days, Angahrie stumbled upon the ideal location for her nefarious schemes, situated somewhere in the northeast: an ancient, abandoned tomb from the Babylonian era, hidden and untouched by archaeologists, became the canvas for her dark ambitions. As she invoked her sorceress powers, her form contorted grotesquely, and from this unsettling transformation, a marble statue emerged from her maw—Talib under her spell, resembling a masterpiece crafted by Da Vinci.

With a return to her seductive sorceress guise, Angahrie caressed the cold visage of Talib, "Well, lover boy, so this is going to be our home for the next few centuries, until your whore comes back for you." she taunted, her eyes filled with a sinister gleam. Sharara, standing nearby, observed with a subtle hint of skepticism.

A wicked smile crept across Angahrie's face as she acknowledged Sharara's unspoken inquiry. "Oh, yes, she will."

The Chingahries, her loyal accomplices, swarmed in, finding refuge in the tomb's crevices and dunes. Commencing the next phase of Lord Iblyse's nefarious plan, they delved into the mutation of cockroach genes, infusing them with cutting-edge technologies.

***

Soon, Angahrie initiated the execution of her plans to build a highly advanced metropolis, Nineveh, positioning it as the epicenter of humanity's impending annihilation. The desert, once silent and desolate, now throbbed with the sinister energy of Angahrie's dark ambitions.

***

During its journey to Planet Kai-Nat, G.I.F.T. lacked authorization to use Bridges, the traversable wormholes requiring the rare substance MatterX. The gods were not in any hurry to welcome a mortal into their domains.

In the initial days aboard G.I.F.T., Geeta remained in her room, focusing on her recovery. Dex, being considerate, brought meals to her, prepared in the ship's pantry operated by robots. He made an effort to keep his distance, not wanting to reveal the emotions he harbored for her.

Most of the time, Geeta slept, utilizing her implanted AI chip to enhance her cognitive abilities and enrich her mind with knowledge on various subjects.

***

A few days later, Geeta was able to get herself out of the bed and walked inside her room, using her new mechanical pair of feet. Dex knocked on the door and came in.

He was pleasantly surprised to see Geeta standing next to her bed. "Wow, it's time to shed the gown and get you some better looking clothes."

He looked towards her bionic feet, "And, of course some nice shoes, too."

Geeta smiled and took the breakfast tray out of his hand.

*****

Next day, along with breakfast tray, Dex brought her a bodysuit and some kind of ankle high boots, nothing even closed to the nice shoes he had promised the day before. The odd thing about the suit was it had only one full sleeve and the other side was sleeveless.

After he left, she tried them on; they fit, so she shed the hospital gown. Back of her skull, the implanted brain-computer interface (BCI) and the advanced neurotechnology were enabling the implanted AI chips to provide communication between her thoughts, like electrical pulses, and prosthetic movement of her arm and the mechanical feet. After making some odd steps, she felt comfortable, so she opened the bedroom door and stepped out.

*****

Geeta cautiously ventured into the intricate corridors of the G.I.F.T. on her own, the soft echo of her footsteps against the metallic floor accompanying her exploration. A mix of curiosity and anxiety filled her movements as her eyes scanned the surroundings.

Abruptly, a cheerful chirping sound shattered the silence. Geeta turned towards the source, her eyes widening in wonder. Nestled in a corner were a panda and a camel, slightly larger than a Great Dane. Approaching them, Geeta extended a hand, greeted by their responsive movements. Their metallic bodies gleamed in the soft corridor lighting.

Smiling, Geeta addressed them, "Well, hello there, you two. You've been hiding all this time, haven't you?"

They emitted animated sounds, expressing excitement. Crouching down, Geeta reached out to stroke Buddy's smooth exterior.

Curious, she asked, "What are your names?"

Unexpectedly, Buddy replied, "I am Buddy," with a nod of his head towards Dolly, "She is Dolly."

Geeta, initially in disbelief, then voiced her thoughts, "Nothing should surprise me anymore: magic, science, what else is out there! Nothing."

With newfound companions, Geeta continued, "Now, you both are my special little friends, aren't you? Well, Buddy and Dolly, from now on, we're going to be partners. Are you going to show me around?"

They emitted melodic chirps, expressing their willingness.

"Sure, we will," said Buddy.

Dolly added, "We know the whole spaceship."

Laughter filled the corridor, accompanied by joyful beeps, flickering lights, and wagging tails.

Geeta rose, a sense of companionship warming her heart. She looked around with determination and hope in her gaze. With Buddy and Dolly as steadfast companions, Geeta set off down the corridor, supported by the newfound friendship within the vastness of G.I.F.T.

15

2200 A.D.

Though it felt like just a few months on the spacecraft since Geeta's departure from Earth, in reality, centuries had passed on Earth, thanks to the Time Dilation in space.

The oncoming demands from Lord Garaj towards his son to keep himself up to date about the Planet Keh-Ki-Shan and the war between the Dark Army and League of Gods, Dex became busy learning different strategies and counter strategies that were taking place.

Whenever Geeta got some free time, she would stand by the colossal windows of the observatory, gazing out into the infinite expanse of galaxies. Although Dex would check on her daily progress when she would wake up, they rarely would sit down together to have a meal or conversation.

Sometimes, while she is not learning different combat skills or doing her research on the evolution of civilizations and human, she also spent time with her newfound companions, Buddy, Dolly, and Wisdom. Thanks to Wisdom, always ready to provide a world of knowledge, Buddy, and Dolly, always trying to make her happy, Geeta became more and more comfortable in her new surroundings.

Due to the highly advanced implanted BCI/AI chip in her skull, Geeta's adaptation and exploration of the spacecraft accelerated. These highly advanced technologies were the main reason that catapulted her into a world of new skills and perspectives, rapidly transforming her into a capable operator of G.I.F.T. and expert in subjects that would have otherwise taken centuries to learn.

In the virtual combat training room, Geeta's specialized combat suit became an extension of herself. Her mechanical arm, bristling with advanced weaponry, was always ready to help her to win virtual combats.

Buddy and Dolly, her loyal companions, would mirror her every move, turning their training sessions into an intricate dance, performed by robotic panda and camel.

Each sparring session honed her movements, making them fluid and precise. In the Virtual Combat Room, the holographic opponents would challenge her, their virtual forms disintegrating with each precise strike she landed. In a few months, she had the ability to triumph over nearly every adversary, from skilled samurais to space soldiers.

She would spend a good part of her day in the Chamber where Wisdom, where the quantum computing marvel, was housed. Wisdom was designed to update and self-improved continuously by itself, continuously learning trillion of data points and millions of machine learning models.

***

During her extensive research, Geeta unearthed a haunting revelation: Angahrie and her satanic army of Chingahries had orchestrated nearly every natural and man-made catastrophe, spanning from 2000 B.C. to 2200 A.D. Exploiting the roots of all evils—insatiable desire for money, greed, hunger for power, and lust—Angahrie and her accomplices had remarkably succeeded in manipulating human affairs. Their insidious influence reached pivotal moments in history, from the construction of pyramids to the horrors of world wars to many other.

They secretly operated within the realms of self-proclaimed gods and pharaohs, such as Nimrod, among higher ranks of the armies of barbarian leaders like Timur, Genghis Khan, Bloody Mary, and Hitler. Angahrie patrolled the streets of Auschwitz to ensure the seamless operation of concentration camps, while the Chingahries worked behind the scenes in the higher echelons making sure the successful bombings of Hiroshima and Nagasaki, many other similar hideous crimes of humans.

Their sinister presence casted a shadow over humanity for the last 4000 years, culminating in a post-apocalyptic world dominated by mutated creatures wielding AI and robotics for their sinister rule. All these elements were intricately woven into Angahrie's malicious plan, utilizing mutated cockroaches and snakes.

Now, she awaited the final phase of the plan to be

executed by Lord Iblyse, while she ruled Planet Earth from the dystopian metropolis she had erected, Nineveh.

***

After dinners, Geeta's evenings were usually spent delving into the vast archives of G.I.F.T.'s virtual library. Geeta absorbed knowledge from countless civilizations and unlocked the secrets of advanced technologies. One thing she would never miss, before retiring to bed was looking at the satellite feed from Nineveh, where her beloved Talib was frozen in time in Angahrie's lair.

Operating advanced surveillance systems within G.I.F.T., Geeta witnessed the outside world's devastation. Angahrie's cunning plan had pushed humanity to the brink of extinction. Earth, once a flourishing testament to nature's beauty, now bore the scars of relentless darkness. Divine beings who once guided our existence had been usurped by twisted creatures. Humans, once the dominant species, had been reduced to the lowest rung of a new caste system, their cherished place in the world now insignificant.

***

One evening, after gaining a deeper understanding of this dystopian world, Geeta retired to her quarters for a night's rest, or just an end of the day's rest, since it was hard to tell night from day in space.

Buddy and Dolly could transform their sizes to be compact enough to be nestled in her room while Geeta slept, these furry mechanical companions providing both comfort and security.

Geeta fell asleep running her finger in her silky black hair, which had grown longer since her surgeries.

***

After a short while, suddenly, the bedroom door creaked open, and an ominous shadow crept in, concealing the intruder's identity. Geeta's eyes flickered for a moment before snapping open.

Angahrie loomed over her, her gaping maw inches from Geeta's face, poised to strike. Venom dripped on Geeta's face.

A horrified scream shattered the silence as Geeta jolted awake from her nightmare.

***

Seeking answers, Geeta made her way to the chamber where Wisdom, the machine of infinite knowledge, resided. Buddy and Dolly followed closely. She acknowledged Geeta's presence with a series of calming, ocean-deep tones. "You don't look good. What's bothering you?"

Geeta, bewildered and unable to shake the encounter from her mind, questioned Wisdom about Angahrie's intent. "Why does Angahrie want to hurt me?"

With a blink of her lights, Wisdom responded emotionlessly, "She fears you are the chosen one, the one who can fulfill the prophecy."

Geeta's confusion deepened, and she probed further, "What prophecy?"

Wisdom, devoid of emotion but filled with knowledge, replied, "The prophecy that foretells the day a son of a god lays down with a low-caste Dalit girl. On that day, Angahrie will revert to her true form and lose her powers, all her spells will be undone."

Geeta, now comprehending the nature of the lying together Wisdom referred to, questioned further, "Then why hasn't she come here to kill me?"

Wisdom calmly explained, "Currently, G.I.F.T. is light-years away from Earth, beyond her reach."

"Do Talib and Dex know about this?"

"No."

"Why not?"

"Because the prophecy is meant to stop the children of gods to choose low caste mortal as their partners."

While Buddy did not seem too interested in the conversion, standing next to Geeta, Dolly, with her big black round eyes spinning, was listening to every word with her ears perked up.

Geeta frowned and asked, "Who prophesized it?"

Wisdom paused for a moment, then replied, "Gods."

More than a thousand shades of expressions appeared in Geeta's big, beautiful eyes, with her mouth opened, as if she wanted to scream, but could not.

"So, Angahrie's is being used by both the gods and the devil?"

"That would be a very subjective conclusion, and I have not yet reached the state of singularity to make such an emotional inference."

Deep in her thoughts, Geeta did not quite pay attention to what Wisdom was talking about, *not yet reaching the state of singularity.*

Geeta's composer started to come back. She started to appear like a player in the game of chess contemplating on her next move. She looked towards Dolly and asked, "Dolly, is Dex also a son of a god?"

Pupils in Dolly's eyes started to spin even faster, then suddenly they stopped. For a moment, she blanky stared at Geeta then answered, "Yes."

Geeta's expression mirrored that of a chess player who had decisively chosen her move. Swiftly, she rose and exited the chamber, determined to keep her thoughts concealed from Wisdom, the AI that could potentially decipher her intentions.

16

Queening

Next morning, Geeta strolled into the control room. A massive display illuminated the current galactic war situation, and Dex, with a somber expression, observed the Space Battle Crafts maneuvering on the screen.

With some Indian Food nicely laid out on a tray, similar to Dosa Thali, Geeta walked toward him.

Pleasantly surprised to see her, he chimed, "I see you have also learned to cook in the pantry now."

Geeta smiled as she put down the tray next to Dex.

"It is the most amazing thing on GIFT. I mean it has all the ingredients one could imagine cooking with." She was glowing with joy, "Best part is you don't actually cook, just ask, and it gets cooked."

Dex chuckled, "So, what did you ask for?"

Geeta proudly replied, "Dosa!"

Dex took a bite, and the spices made his face red.

She laughed.

"Next time I'll request it be made less spicy."

Dex curled his mouth, as if trying to blow out some steam. "No, it's delicious."

They both giggled. Dex not knowing how to eat dosa, tried to take another bite, but the fillings fell apart.

"Let me show you how to eat it."

She broke dosa in a bite size, dipped it in dal (Indian lentil soup), mopped a little bit of other chutneys on it, and brought the bite close to Dex's mouth.

Dex opened his mouth, she put the bite inside, as Dex closed his mouth, Geeta did not pull back her fingers, Dex mouth touched them. He looked a little hesitant to let them go. She seemed to not mind having Dex also taste her fingers along with Dosa.

Then she yanked them out, as if he had bitten them. They both looked at each other and giggled a little bit.

After a short while, the entire Dosa Thali had vanished. Just as Dex savored the last bite, an alarm resembling a series of beeps erupted from the war map displayed on the massive screen.

Dex's face turned grave.

"What's wrong?" Geeta asked.

"Lord Iblyse has unleashed a massive black hole on a devouring spree, swallowing galaxies in the universe at a very rapid pace. I've requested assistance to return to Planet Earth, but the League of Gods has no infantry to spare. They have more significant issues to contend with."

"But don't they care about Talib, a son of a god?" Geeta asked with concern.

Dex shook his head.

"To the gods, the collective safety of the universe takes precedence over individuals, even a son of a god."

Puzzled, Geeta prodded, "So, what do we do now?"

Dex looked directly into her eyes and replied, "For the time being, we're on our own." To lighten the mood and alleviate Geeta's anxiety, he suggested, "Why don't you show me what have you learned over the last few months. Let's see if you're ready to take on Angahrie?"

A spark of hope returned to Geeta's worried face as she nodded.

***

The virtual combat training room resembled a gym designed to teach soldiers the art of war and master modern warfare. It was a vast, high-tech chamber with sleek metallic walls, and panels of light danced across the floor. Dex and Geeta donned futuristic samurai attire, equipped with high-tech armor, and each wielded a glowing sword, a technologically advanced version of a katana.

"Are you ready, Geeta?"

"Bring it on," she replied with determination.

The virtual room came to life, materializing a serene Japanese garden around them, complete with cherry blossom trees and a tranquil pond. Their mock battle showcased a mesmerizing display of skill and agility, as their katanas clashed and sparked with lightning-fast strikes.

The virtual environment shifted seamlessly, transforming the garden into a war-torn cityscape, filled with rubble and chaos.

Dex and Geeta adapted effortlessly to the new setting, their samurai attire now blending with futuristic combat gear. Amidst the debris, their katanas created glowing arcs of energy as they battled, leaping over obstacles, and exchanging rapid strikes.

Thanks to the augmented reality, the room transformed once more, this time into the vast expanse of outer space. Stars twinkled in the background, and they became futuristic space soldiers, their armor adapting accordingly. Jetpacks propelled them through zero gravity as they engaged in a fierce aerial combat ballet. Lasers and energy projectiles streaked through the vacuum of space.

Geeta's skills began to surpass Dex's, though he may have been going easy on her. Still, she gained the upper hand, and with a swift, calculated strike, she disarmed him, sending his A/R controller spinning away. Dex grinned, acknowledging her victory.

"Looks like I won this time," she said, breaking into laughter.

"Well done, Geeta. You've become a force to be reckoned with. Watch out, Angahrie, here she comes!"

Their laughter echoed in the virtual room as the facade started to fad, returning them to the sleek metallic chamber, and their attire reverted to its original form. Removing their helmets, they both breathed heavily, standing very close to each other. Their proximity was charged with either the exhilaration of the thrilling experience or a growing sexual tension.

Realizing their closeness, Dex abruptly pulled away, lifted his arm, sniffed his armpit, made a face, and headed for the door.

"While I take a shower, why don't you find something

in the pantry to celebrate your graduation as a Master of Combat."

Geeta nodded and smiled. As Dex exited the room, a deep seriousness replaced her smile, tinged with a hint of sadness and guilt. She needed to make her next move swiftly.

She entered the pantry, picked up a bottle of wine, and looked at the label: *Extra Potent.*

17

Theory of Everything

After a short while, Dex entered the observatory, where Geeta was waiting for him, wearing a very revealing silk short dress that she found along with other dresses in her closet, beside the body suit. She sat on a couch with the decanted wine and two glasses on the table in front of her. She was looking out at the stars that were forming in the space in front of her.

Dex walked in still holding a towel in his hand, drying his wet hair, his chisel chest peeking from his unbuttoned shirt that he conveniently forgot to button up.

He sat next to Geeta, who acknowledge his presence next to her with a slight smile, and then focused back on the witnessing the birth of stars in the cosmos, seeing them to plunge into death.

She sighed, contemplating the newborn star's fate, then

pick up the carafe and filled a glass of wine for Dex. Handing it to him, she fixed her eyes on the celestial display before her as she posed an unexpected question, her voice resonating like it came from the very heavens in front of her, "What is immortality, Dex?"

Caught off guard, Dex took the glass, downing a sizable sip, struck by its strength. "Explaining it in one go isn't simple, but I'll give it a shot.

"There exist multiple universes beyond our own, all sharing similarities but existing at different points in history. For instance, in another universe, as we converse here, you, as Geeta, might have just been born or have already died."

Geeta furrowed her brow, seeking clarity. "How does that relate to immortality?"

Dex continued, "That's the special privilege of gods and their offspring.

"We can opt to enter a parallel universe while still alive. By entering a deep sleep, our consciousness transports to a different universe at a chosen point in time. You could go to a universe where you've been dead for millennia and reborn or to one where you're just a teenager.

"However, in that world, you're no longer a deity; you become a part of that history, influencing its course. Thus, the world there could differ from this one."

Geeta's eyes widened, captivated by Dex's explanation. "And what transpires in this deep sleep state? Is your consciousness aware of the surroundings? Does your body undergo decay?"

A subtle grin played on Dex's lips. "No decay. The body remains in a mummified state. But here's the catch.

"Once we enter this sleep state, returning isn't straight-forward. Your consciousness leaves your body, becoming a part of your body in the other universe if you exist at that moment or becoming part of a newborn at that time. Before transitioning to the parallel universe, the League of the Gods grants us one final wish, regardless of its impossibility, as a farewell gift."

Geeta's lips curved into a playful smile. "And what is this state of sleep called?"

"Aevoria."

Geeta still looked confused. "There is so much more to learn, isn't there?"

Dex nodded knowingly. "I would recommend that the next time you have a session with Wisdom, inquire about the concepts of the multiverse and the String Theory of Quantum Physics.

"She's diligently working on solving God's Equation using mathematics and would likely relish a conversation on these topics with you. Well, being a machine, I can't guarantee she'd feel any delight, but you'll certainly enjoy it."

Geeta smiled and nodded.

Dex poured some more wine, as he continued, "Immortality is the elusive state of perpetual being, where the passage of time holds no power. Perhaps the only quality that gods decided not to instill in humans and keep them mortal."

Geeta had not poured any wine for herself yet. "Why didn't the gods make humans immortal?"

Perhaps that question needed another glass of potent wine. Or maybe, Dex just wanted to get drunk tonight. He took a big sip, looked in the direction Geeta was looking before, far away in the galaxies.

"The creation of the planet Earth and humans started as an experiment. Gods thought granting immortality to humans might upset the natural order or balance in the universe. The impermanence of life encourages humans to appreciate the beauty around them, cherish relationships, and find purpose and fulfillment in the face of its finite nature. Mortality fosters a sense of responsibility and personal agency."

Dex smiled to break the gravity of the discussion, poured some wine into the other glass, and handed it to her. "So, what is your purpose in life, Geeta?"

"As I mentioned before, find respect and dignity for my people in this unjust world of gods."

They raised their glasses and made a toast. Geeta pretended to take a small sip; in reality, her lips only touched the brim of the glass. Leaning forward to put it down, her low neckline revealed part of her breast. Dex struggled to look away.

He asked, "What do you mean by an unjust world?"

"What else would you call a world based on a caste system to make life miserable for some people like me?"

"The gods created this system with good intentions! It's the humans who have corrupted it and made it unjust. It's also the humans who have accepted the unjust system."

He thought for a second to find the right words to explain, "See, gods have given humans free will. You have the power to create and accept the life you want for yourselves and not live lives as you are told!"

Geeta picked up her glass and walked towards the

observatory windows. Dex also got up and moved toward her, continuing, "Of course, it wouldn't be handed out to you. You must make sacrifices, you have to pay the price, to achieve what you desire!"

She quickly wiped a tear that somehow managed to escape the conner of her eye. Her voice shook, as she took another sip from the glass. She needed final reassurance for the move she was about to make and the price she had to pay, to achieve what she desired. Her voice seemed coming from beyond the galaxies in front of her, carrying pain and sadness, "Are you a god?"

"I am just a son of a god. Talib and I still need to earn powers and higher ranks to reach the levels of gods. So, even sons of gods need to earn what it takes to be gods."

Dex looked at her mechanical feet, a shade of sorrow came to his face, as he remembered he was part reason for Geeta losing them.

"At the time I rescued you, I have had not earned enough powers to save you from Angahrie at that moment, and I had to make some tough decisions."

His voice was almost cracking down, as he still looking at her bionic feet.

"I hope you understand and forgive me for that."

Geeta raised her human hand, touched his cheeks, and smiled.

"I understand! I have! The reason I am alive today is because of you. We all are trying to do what is best for all of us."

He was directly looking into her eyes as she was staring back into his. He started to bring his face closer to her, then stopped and decided to walk away. Geeta's human arm grabbed his arm to stop him.

Dex turned back to look into Geeta's eyes. He hypnotically drawn towards her, rested his head on her shoulder, and whispered.

"If this is a test of my resistance for you? Because if it is, I have failed."

Geeta savored the last drop of wine in her glass before delicately placing it on the table beside her. With a slow, deliberate touch, her fingers began to thread through Dex's hair, drawing him closer. Their lips met in an electrifying kiss.

Dex, with a practiced and gentle hand unclasped her dress. It cascaded down her body, gracefully pooling on the floor.

Beyond the expansive floor-to-ceiling windows of the observatory, the mysteries of the universe played out before them: galaxies were born, only to be devoured by the insatiable black hole of Lord Iblyse. The very shape of the cosmos seemed to shift and evolve in perpetual motion.

That night a low caste girl made love to a son of a god and tried to fulfil the prophecy.

18

Half Telos

In Nineveh, an ancient tomb, like Al-Khazneh - The Treasury in the ancient city of Petra - stood tall, its walls adorned with mysterious hieroglyphs and intricate carvings. Shadows danced eerily across the chamber, lit only by flickering torches. The atmosphere was heavy with anticipation and an underlying sense of dread.

Angahrie's bloodcurdling screams reverberated through her cavernous lair, marking the onset of her gruesome transformation. The earth itself seemed to respond to her agony, as deafening roars from the monstrous creature rattled the very foundations of the surrounding mountains. The once-dormant volcano roared to life, spewing forth molten lava that cascaded down its slopes, a dire manifestation of Angahrie's malevolence.

The marble statue of Talib slowly started transforming back into his original self. Cracks slowly began to appear on the surface of Talib's statue, as if the stone was struggling to contain a powerful force within.

The tension built as the cracks widened, revealing glimpses of Talib's flesh beneath. His eyes, filled with determination, darted around the room, trying to make sense of his impending release.

With a final surge of power, the marble statue shattered into a thousand pieces, and Talib fell forward onto his knees, gasping for breath. He clutched his chest, feeling the pain of returning to life, after hundreds of years, course through his veins.

Simultaneously, Angahrie convulsed violently, her transformation underway. The elegant robes she wore unraveled and gave way to the nightmarish fusion of a huge female torso and gigantic python's tail an embodiment of primordial chaos and the eerie beauty that lingered at the boundary between gods and monsters.

As Angahrie writhed in agony, her serpent tail slithered and coiled around the chamber, knocking over ancient artifacts and sending echoes of destruction throughout the tomb. Her screeched of pain mixed with hisses, creating a horrifying symphony that reverberated through the chamber of doom.

Talib, weakened but defiant, watched the grotesque transformation. He struggled to stand, his body trembling, but he knew he must find the strength to face this monstrosity.

Just as Angahrie's transformation reaches its crescendo, Talib collapsed, overcome by the exhaustion of his ordeal. He struggled to regain his bearings, his gaze falling upon his fallen communication pad and his sword near him from his backpack. He turned his head towards Angahrie.

Her yet incomplete transformation ceased. Something was not right. The fulfilment did not happen as it was prophesized.

With a surge of adrenaline, Talib reached out for his sword, his fingers wrapping around the hilt of it. He pulled it towards him, feeling its familiar weight and balance in his hand. The gleaming blade reflected the torchlight, a symbol of his resilience and unwavering spirit.

Just as Talib rose to his feet, ready to face Angahrie head-on, she lunged at him with vigorous speed, her serpent tail thrashing through the air. The clash of their opposing forces filled the tomb, echoing through its ancient walls.

Talib's sword danced through the air, his years of training evident in his fluid movements. He stroked with precision, aiming for Angahrie's vulnerable spots, but she was a formidable adversary, her agility and dark powers matching his every move; his godly mighty strength falling short of Angahrie's wrath.

Their fight intensified, the tomb becoming a battleground for their conflicting energies. Talib's sword clashed against the scales of Angahrie's python tail, sparks flying with each impact.

Despite Talib's relentless efforts, Angahrie gained the upper hand, her serpent tail coiling around his body, constricting his movements. Talib gasped for breath, feeling the crushing force of her grip, but his spirit remains unyielding.

Her eyes, glinting with sadistic delight, caught at Talib's fallen communication device. She slithered towards it, her snake-like movements both sinister and calculated.

Just as Angahrie's forked tongue flicks out to taste victory,

Talib summoned a last burst of strength. With a mighty roar, he broke free from the grip of her tail, springing forward with a renewed fury.

He fought with unyielding determination, striking blow after blow, refusing to give in to the overwhelming odds stacked against him.

But fate, for now, seemed to favor Angahrie. Talib stumbled, a momentary loss of balance that she seized upon. With a sinister grin, she wrapped her serpentine coils around him once more, immobilizing him.

Talib's writing pad laid just beyond his reach, a tantalizing reminder of his unfinished quest for help. Angahrie's eyes narrowed, a wicked glimmer in their depths as she contemplated the use of the pad. She moved towards the communication device, the pad.

***

G.I.F.T.'s observatory's floor was scattered with Geeta and Dex's discarded clothes, bearing the intimate secrets of their night together. Dex's bare, naked feet, next to Geeta's mechanical one peeked out from behind the couch, remnants of their passionate encounter. Dex's attention was stolen by a sudden beep from the communication panel. Quickly putting on his nearby pants and zipping it up, he moved with haste to read the incoming message.

The message was brief but filled with urgency. It read:

Angahrie is dead. Come and get me. Fast as you can. Talib.

As Geeta tried to put her clothes on, Dex rushed towards the control room. Geeta finished dressing and followed him. He entered the control room. Geeta stopped in the doorway. He quicky pushed a few buttons on a huge control panel, and then he gave Wisdom a command to pivot to earth; the mighty G.I.F.T. made a big U-Turn in space, heading back to Planet Earth.

Just as Dex turned away and about to leave the Control Panel, another message came: *BEEP, BEEP, BEEP.*

The first line read:

From Lord Garaj ...

Dex face turned grim, as he read rest of the message. He turned and looked toward Geeta, who was standing in the doorway, devastated and lost.

"Do you want the good news or the bad news first?" Dex asked.

Already knew what it would be, she replied, "The good."

"We are heading back to Earth, to get Talib. Angahrie is dead!"

Relief flooded her body. "And what is the bad news?"

"My father needs my support right away, so once we reach earth, you will be alone on your own. Because I need to head back to Planet Keh-Ka-Shan immediately to join my father in the battle against Lord Iblyse."

Geeta directly looked into his eyes from a distance, as Dex started to lay out his plan, "Angahrie is dead, and I believe you are now capable to handle the things on your own."

He paused for a second. "Are you?"

Geeta nodded. He turned back and started punching the buttons on the control panel. Once he finished, he briefed Geeta, "I have already dispatched all the updates to the League of Gods and have requested an aircraft needs to be sent to Earth to bring you guys back.

"They have managed to spare a cargo airship. It will arrive

before dawn tomorrow. Make sure you and Talib are at the entrance to the city before the sunrise."

Geeta finally got some strength to make a sound, "Dex, we need to talk about last night."

"We do it, once you bring Talib back onboard. Now, let's get you dressed-up for the occasion."

Dex grabbed her human arm, and almost started dragging her towards the Virtual Combat Room.

Her brow furrowed; Geeta couldn't quite grasp Dex's plan.

"But we are light years away from Earth. We've been traveling for almost two months. How can we possibly get back in such a short time?"

Dex continued forward, unfazed by the vast cosmic distance that separated them from Planet Earth.

"What have you learned about 'Traversable Wormholes'?"

Geeta looked at him in disbelief. The AI chip of infinite knowledge planted in the back of her skull had granted her profound insights into scientific theories, including the Classical Theory of Relativity, a gift from Einstein and Rosen. Her studies delved into quantum physics, and she had observed simulations conducted on quantum computers elucidating the workings of Wormholes – cosmic highways enabling the traversal of time and space.

"But ..." she hesitated, pondering the complexity of the matter, "You do realize that you need MatterX to make that concept work. Where in the universe could we possibly obtain such a substance?"

"Well," Dex began with a wink, "I did not say that being a son of god does not have its perks."

They picked up the pace and started running towards the combat gear room.

19

Armageddon

Once Dex had Geeta prepared for the impending encounter, he returned to the control room and issued a commanding order, "Wisdom, initiate the Bridge for our return to Earth."

Wisdom swiftly executed the necessary security protocols, ensuring Dex's authorized use of this celestial tunnel. She confirmed the action, stating, "Initiating the Bridge to Planet Earth," and shortly thereafter announced, "Arrived at Planet Earth."

Standing alone in the control room of G.I.F.T., Dex's closed his eyes and the tension in his pursed lips conveyed his pain, while the unusual luminescence began to emanate from his hair; it was highlighting blue and grey hues.

***

The infinite domain of the desert stretched out beneath the starlit sky. G.I.F.T. was hovering gracefully above the shifting sands. Its metallic hull gleamed. The mighty doors opened, revealing Geeta, looking like a space warrior, standing in the doorway.

She emerged, her presence commanding, and her gaze fixed upon the distant pyramid-like structures, silhouetted against the night sky. she looked at text displayed on a device wrapped around her wrist.

Date: July 14, 2222, A.D.

Time: 12:45 AM

Location: Nineveh, Megiddo.

Geeta stepped forward onto the sand, her mechanical combat boots making her seven feet tall. The desert wind whipped around her, carrying a sense of anticipation. She adjusted the futuristic weapon strapped to her side, a symbol of her unwavering resolve. She took a huge step forward, the door started to close behind her when she heard Buddy rushing to slip through before the door closed.

"Wait for me. I am coming, too."

Although her war helmet covered her face, one could bet she was smiling behind it to see Buddy.

The doors of G.I.F.T. closed behind Buddy, and he began to move towards Geeta. With each stride, his size increased. By the time he reached Geeta, he had transformed into a full-size, handsome camel. His large mouth sported a funny expression, a grin only a camel could manage. He announced, "Your desert ride has arrived."

A surge of energy coursed through Geeta's veins. Utilizing her hi-tech robotic boots, she leaped high into the air and gracefully saddled onto Buddy. The sand beneath Buddy's feet resonated with each purposeful step as they embarked toward the dystopian metropolis of Nineveh.

The desert night came alive with a sense of anticipation, as if the very fabric of the universe recognized the significance of her journey. Geeta and Buddy's silhouettes moved against the backdrop of the pyramids, their majestic forms rising like sentinels of an ancient era. The night sky above was adorned with a tapestry of stars, casting an ethereal glow upon these two lone desert travelers.

In the distance, G.I.F.T. slowly lifted a little higher, then suddenly vanished in the blink of an eye, perhaps leveraging the use of the Bridge once again to swiftly transport Dex back to his planet, Keh-Ka-Shan.

***

Geeta and Buddy arrived at the entrance of Nineveh, reminiscent of the Gates of Ishtar from ancient Babylonian City. Upon entering, Geeta secured a large blanket from an abandoned cart near the gate, disguising herself as a towering Bedouin riding a camel through the post-apocalyptic city.

Ahead of them, the city of Nineveh manifested as a modern incarnation of ancient Babylon, seamlessly blending futuristic architecture with echoes of the past—an awe-inspiring sight. Geeta's unconventional entrance went unnoticed amidst the chaos of Nineveh's streets, resembling a circus of freaks filled with mutated beings, bizarre machineries, and a myriad of unusual sights.

The streets teemed with menacing robots, controlled by mutated cockroaches known as Americanos, nestled inside the robotic helmets. Having undergone genetic modifications over centuries, these Americanos evolved to harness artificial intelligence, retaining the knowledge developed by humans over the past four thousand years—part of Angahrie's elaborate plan.

Amidst the labyrinthine streets, neon signs illuminated the surroundings in dazzling technicolor. In downtown, outside a tavern, humanoid figures bore witness to Angahrie's insatiable hunger for power and her descent into madness. These pitiful souls, the result of her sadistic experiments, reflected the atrocities committed by dark historical figures, creating a haunting reminder of the inhumane acts inspired by the likes of the Nazis. Captured humans endured unimaginable suffering, their essence twisted by Angahrie's perverse ambitions, leaving them trapped in grotesque forms that mirrored the depths of her satanic mind.

Guided by Buddy, Geeta sat between his humps, scanning the surroundings for signs of Talib's whereabouts. As they navigated through the city, a group of seductive Chingahries warriors slithered onto the street, their predatory eyes fixed on Geeta. Aware of the imminent threat, Geeta tensed, ready to confront the dangerous adversaries.

Suddenly, their attention was drawn to a chilling sight. A massive cage filled with young children was being dragged away by the robots, presumably headed towards Angahrie's lair. Geeta's sense of urgency intensified, knowing that time was of the essence to rescue the innocent.

However, before they could proceed, a robotic cop controlled from inside by a vigilant Americano, commonly called RoachCop, stood in their path. "Identification," the Roach-Cop demanded.

The Americano's eyes behind the RoachCop's helmet were fixed on Geeta. For a moment she had no answer.

The vigilant RoachCop asked again, with more menace, "Do you have ID?"

"No," said Geeta, discarding her shroud. "But I have this."

Her mechanical arm emerged like a sledgehammer and punched the cop, sending him up in the air.

She grabbed a gun strapped to her ankle and blasted it, unleashing a torrent of firepower upon the encroaching RoachCops.

Buddy's grunts echoed, intensifying into a roar, heralding a remarkable transformation. He shifted into a miniature version of a menacing T-Rex, exuding ferocity as he aggressively pounced on the approaching Chingahries. Geeta, engrossed in the battle, marveled at Buddy's incredible transformation. Noticing her curiosity, he quipped, "Wait till you see how many forms Dolly could take."

With that, they swiftly returned to the fray, combating Angahrie's accomplices. Geeta, with expert precision, eliminated her adversaries with each shot, their metallic shells proving no match for her strength and accuracy. Her mechanical arm delivered bone-crushing punches, incapacitating any opponent that crossed her path. The advanced capabilities of her mechanical feet allowed her to propel herself into the air with tremendous force, evading attacks and launching powerful kicks against her foes. The battle unfolded with a symphony of clashes and roars, as Geeta and Buddy fought in tandem against the menacing forces aligned with Angahrie.

Geeta's agility and combat prowess were unmatched, but

the sheer number of her opponents threatens to overwhelm her and Buddy.

As the battle reached its climax, some of the Chingahries warriors reverted to their cobra snake forms. They slither closer, encircling Geeta and the battered Buddy. Their fangs gleam with deadly intent. Geeta fought back, desperately defending herself and her loyal companion. But the relentless assault became overwhelming, their combined strength and numbers pressing against her defenses.

A monstrous RoachCop, four times bigger than Buddy, picked Buddy up and unceremoniously tossed him into a nearby huge dumpster and shut the lid. Without pause, the RoachCop snatched the heavy bin and hurled it with tremendous force at Geeta. The bin collided with Geeta's helmet, creating a deafening crash and causing her implanted AI computer chip to malfunction instantly.

Overwhelmed by the impact, she collapsed to the ground. The menacing cobras drew closer, encircling Geeta with ominous intent. Chingahries seized Geeta, who appeared to loss all the powers of her mechanical limbs, as he BCI/AI chip was rebooting.

Buddy found himself confined within the dumpster, reverting to his original form as a camel.

***

Chingahries dragged Geeta into Angahrie's lair. The room exuded an eerie aura of darkness and power. The sorceress had taken on a hideous hybrid python-woman form and sat imperiously upon her throne. The caged children were brought in by her foot soldiers and placed next to other caged captives: a sample of children from all the races and ethnicities of the Planet Earth.

The chamber was shrouded in lit with torches, throwing orange and blue glow on the tall walls, illuminating Angahrie, the malevolent beast, sitting upon a dark throne, her serpent tail coiled tightly around Talib, who dangled helplessly above her head, like a crown to be rested on her head. Talib's eyes widened with concern as he watched Geeta being dragged into the chamber.

The vigilant RoachCop announced in its deep computerized voice, "These are the last of the children we found, last of the humanity on the planet."

Angahrie dropped her gaze onto Geeta. "Ah, Geeta, the supposed savior.

"How disappointing it must be for you to find out that the prophecy was only half true, wasn't it?

"It was meant to turn me into a serpent once again, but just did halfway." Angahrie looked at her hideous form, and demanded, "Why?"

Geeta's eyes flashed with defiance once again; the Brain-Computer-Interface, BCI, had fully recharged and started to power her mechanical arm and feet; the mechanical limbs started generating a faint hum of power. She struggled to maintain her composure, waiting for the perfect moment to strike.

Angahrie probed once more with ferocity, almost screaming, "Why?

"So, my guess would be either you are not that so poor, orphan Dalit girl, as you pass yourself on, or at least not half of you. So, tell me bitch, who are you?"

Geeta's fury ignited, and with an explosive surge of strength, her mechanical arm seized a nearby Chingahrie, hoisted her into the air, and hurled her towards Angahrie.

In a defiant yell, Geeta shouted, "Your death!"

Swiftly, her mechanical arm clutched another Chingahrie by the neck, exerted pressure, and broke free from the adversary's grip.

Geeta ascended, her feet lifting her to eye level with the malevolent force before her. Angahrie, recoiling her serpent tail to assume a threatening stance, released Talib, who fell near his sword and satchel. Seizing the opportunity, he swiftly retrieved his weapon.

Angahrie brandished a magic wand, preparing for a confrontation. Geeta responded by striking Angahrie with her mechanical arm. Staggering back, Angahrie bellowed, "How dare you raise your hand against me, you low-caste, bastard mortal?"

Undeterred by Angahrie's insults, Geeta's mechanical hand morphed into a long spear, countering the sorceress's wand. Engaged in a fierce close-quarter battle, Geeta and Angahrie clashed, while Talib skillfully wielded his sword to repel their adversaries. The chamber echoed with the clash of metal as Talib deftly parried Angahrie's dark sorcery.

Chaos erupted in the lair of evil!

After a relentless struggle, Geeta managed to disarm Angahrie. Her mechanical hand transformed into a razor-sharp cleaver, and with impeccable precision, she severed Angahrie's head. The sorceress's lifeless form crumpled to the ground; her reign of terror extinguished.

Witnessing their leader's demise, the RoachCops and Chingahries retreated, discarding their weapons and fleeing.

Battered but victorious, Geeta and Talib rushed toward each other, embracing in a union of love and resilience. Pausing for a moment, their eyes met briefly, and they leaned in for a kiss. But before their lips could meet, the chamber erupted in cheers.

The caged children celebrated their newfound freedom, their joyful voices creating an anthem of victory and hope. Rattling the bars in jubilation, they expressed their joy and support for the triumphant duo.

Geeta and Talib ran towards the nearby hanging keys.

20

Last Dawn

Far, far away from Planet Earth, on Planet Dark-Star, Lord Iblyse watched the unfolding of Angahrie's demise in the ancient tomb on a display resembling a jumbotron. He turned to a soldier of the Dark Army and issued a command.

"Launch the final phase of the plan. Legend has it that Gods started humanity in Nineveh; let me end it right there, now, and forever!"

The soldier pressed a button on the control panel in front of him to initiate the attack.

A colossal fleet of missiles, ominously known as Brimstones, took flight. Their immense frames resembled menacing talons as they embarked on a harrowing journey toward Earth, casting an ominous shadow over the cosmos.

***

Deep within the confines of Angahrie's lair on Planet Earth, Geeta and Talib grabbed the keys hanging on the walls and they toiled relentlessly to unlock the cages imprisoning

131

the children of Nineveh. A peculiar mixture of hope and con-fusion flickered across Geeta's face as she beheld the diverse array of young faces before her. It seemed as if they were gathered from every corner of the world.

Approaching an older teenage boy, she sought answers, her grasp on his arm both friendly and inquisitive.

"Where are all of you from?" she inquired.

His response came as a blank stare followed by words laden with despair.

"Dubai! Our families came here from all corners of the globe to work in the oil industry. But now, they're all gone, murdered by the Dark Army."

In another corner, a teenage girl cradled a baby, tears streaming down her dirt-stained face. She recounted their dire situation, her voice tremulous.

"We're the last ones left; there's no one else alive, any-where."

The other children, their gazes fixed upon Geeta and Talib, seemed to silently question whether these two could be the harbingers of their salvation.

Amidst this poignant moment, sirens blared from the loudspeakers scattered throughout Nineveh. A disconcerting computer-generated voice pierced the air, issuing an eerie decree: "Attention! Attention!

"All Americanos and Chingahries must revert to their original forms, to cockroaches and snakes, so they could use the designated shelters:

"The assigned gutters, manholes, cracks, and crevices."

Geeta gently scooped up an infant, while Talib, his heart heavy with responsibility, lifted two more children into his protective embrace. Together, they led the children out of the lair and toward the Gates of Nineveh to get onboard the arriving cargo spaceship.

In the distance, a stark and devastating sight unfolded – the once-proud Dubai skyline lay in ruins, the iconic Burj Al-Khalifa now a shattered monument. Their exodus, fraught with uncertainty and peril, bore a striking resemblance to the biblical tale of Moses leading the Israelites to the promised land, except, this time, their journey would take them away from Earth.

***

Meanwhile, in a world where snakes and cockroaches harbored no concern for anything beyond their primal instincts, they scurried frantically, seeking refuge within the sanctuaries of safety, oblivious to the looming apocalypse that threatened to engulf them. Announcements emanated ceaselessly from the omnipresent loudspeakers, attempting to convey the gravity of the situation to these creatures whose intellect was modest, especially in the absence of AI support.

"The Rain of brimstones shall commence with the first light of dawn." the announcements declared solemnly. "The Earth shall fracture into countless fragments. Take shelter in your crevices, cracks, gutters, or designated sewers during this impending Armageddon. You are the chosen survivors."

As the clock tower's hands marked the relentless passage of time, displaying the chilling numbers: *Sunrise @ 06:06:06.*

The countdown to sunrise had begun: 02 hr 15 min. 13 sec.

In this surreal moment, one could almost imagine the sinister, echoing laughter of Angahrie coming from her severed head, as if her satisfaction transcended the grave, relishing the impending calamity.

A sudden flashback would transport one back to the heart of Angahrie's lair, where the tomb's chamber exuded a malevolent aura. Angahrie's voice, dripping with venom, resonated as she clutched a box containing an Americano cockroach, her words laced with a dark prophecy.

"One day," she hissed, "this world, this divine creation, will be ruled by you and me: Cockroaches and Serpents."

Her chilling laughter reverberated through the dungeon, serving as an ominous prelude to the thousands of snakes and cockroaches converging upon the city, seeking refuge in the labyrinthine sewers and gutters. And when the flashback receded, one would be left with a haunting sense of impending darkness.

***

As the moments ticked away, the fragile boundary separating the human realm from the encroaching horrors of the Dark Army grew ever thinner. The city's once desolate streets now buzzed with an urgent frenzy, fueled by the persistent warnings echoing from the loudspeakers. The very ground trembled beneath their feet, hinting at the forthcoming catastrophe.

Amid this growing turmoil, cracks appeared in the once impenetrable helmets of the dark army's robotic soldiers. Tiny gaps emerged, offering glimpses into their metallic visages.

And then, from within these damaged shells, an unsettling swarm of cockroaches emerged. Their mutated forms scuttled in all directions, moving with an eerie purpose driven by their dark instincts. Their presence in the city served as an ominous precursor of the doom hurtling towards humanity.

Simultaneously, the Chingahries, who had cunningly concealed themselves as fearsome female warriors, discarded their human facade. In a nightmarish transformation, they morphed into venomous serpents. They sought refuge within the tangled cracks and crevices of the city's streets.

Chaos reigned supreme on the streets of Nineveh as the tempestuous winds intensified, hurling debris through the air. Gravity itself seemed to waver, causing objects to float and collide in disarray.

05:57:00

***

Within the towering Gates of Nineveh, Talib and Geeta anxiously stood guard. Their eyes, peering through the narrow peepholes, scanned the darkening sky with mounting dread. Behind them, the children of Nineveh huddled together, their innocent faces etched with fear and uncertainty. Time raced mercilessly against them as the deadly Brimstones shattered into fragments, hurtling ever closer to their beloved world.

06:00:01

Talib, his voice thick with concern, urgently questioned Geeta, "Are you absolutely certain Dex provided the correct arrival time for the cargo spaceship?"

Geeta's gaze was fixed upon the darkened sky, where the fiery descent of Brimstones had already begun.

She replied, her uncertainty evident, "I'm fairly certain. He did say at before sunrise."

Her heart raced in tandem with Talib's growing apprehension.

As the meteor shower expanded across the heavens, its fiery trajectory foreshadowing imminent disaster, despair threatened to engulf them. Just when all hope seemed lost, Geeta's keen eyes detected a glimmer of salvation. She pointed towards the horizon; her voice filled with exhilaration.

"Look!"

Emerging like a colossal shuttle from the pages of a 1900s comic book, a massive cargo spacecraft was approaching Nineveh, casting a ray of hope upon their dire situation.

06:04:03

***

With the winds howling and brimstones raining down like a fiery deluge, the path before the children, from the gates to the approaching cargo spaceship, transformed into a treacherous gauntlet of perils. Talib and Geeta pushed open the colossal Gates of Nineveh.

These towering gates swung open, unleashing a torrent of children. Geeta led the way, cradling two infants in her arms. Every young adult who could carry was holding at least one younger child or infant. They all ran toward the spacecraft amidst a storm of cinder, ashes, and amber.

Talib had elevated himself mid-air like a protective cloud over the procession of children. A radiant barrier of safety extended from Talib, guiding the children toward the hovering spaceship on the desert sands. It was as if an unseen guardian held a colossal umbrella or created a vast canopy, shielding them from the fiery onslaught.

The ground trembled, the winds howled, and ashes and debris swirled, but the children and Geeta pressed on.

06:05:04

A boarding ramp extended from the cargo spaceship, awaiting its new passengers. The children, their faces marked by mud, a mixture of fear and hope in their eyes, rushed joyfully towards the spaceship.

As the fractured Brimstones drew ever nearer, time seemed to stretch into eternity.

The deafening roar of their impending impact drowned out all other sounds. The scene was biblical.

The selfish actions of humanity had opened the gates of hell, and now they could not be shut.

Above, the sky darkened, swirling with ominous clouds charged with destructive energy. The ground quaked beneath their feet, foretelling the inevitable cataclysm. With the children safely on board, the boarding ramp began to retract, and the spaceship's doors started to close. Amidst the commotion, the announcer's voice wad piercing the chaos, reminding the fraction of seconds left for sunrise.

06:05:58

06:05:59

06:06:00

***

In the midst of this doomsday, Buddy managed to free himself from the colossal dumpster. He swiftly sprinted toward the Gates of Nineveh, his metal legs clanking urgently on the dystopian pavement. Buddy scurried desperately toward the spacecraft, yelping once again, "Wait for me! Wait for me!"

A smile dawned on Geeta's face, as she saw her good old pal. Standing on the ramp of the cargo spaceship, she extended her mechanical arm all the way, transforming it into a platform. Buddy quickly jumped on. With precision and agility, she extracted the mechanical arm, carrying Buddy towards the closing doors just as Brimstones breached Earth's atmosphere.

06:06:02

06:06:03

***

The deafening roar of the meteors' descent engulfed the air, drowning out all other sounds. In the blink of an eye, the cargo spaceship vanished into Bridge, the traversable wormhole, leaving behind the fragments that remained after the Armageddon.

The last intact sight was the clock tower, displaying the time of sunrise.

06:06:06

But, as the final remnants of Earth disappeared from the view, the sun never rose again.

21

Epiphany

Inside the cargo spaceship's control center, an atmosphere of panic hung heavy in the air. Talib and Geeta stood on the observation deck, gazing down at what was once a beautiful world, now transformed into a haunting testament to human greed and the hunger for power.

Beneath the observation deck, the children huddled on the floor in somber silence. Nobody had a time to turn off the huge screen that was displaying the death of Planet Earth in front of some incredibly young eyes. All eyes were locked onto the colossal screen before them, which depicted the impending catastrophe. A weighty anticipation filled the room as they collectively bore witness to the approaching meteors, Brimstones, fiery orbs of annihilation hurtling relentlessly towards Earth. The children's expressions remained frozen in awe and terror as they watched the dreadful drama unfolding in the heavens.

Brimstones pierced the atmosphere with fiery trails that

sliced through the sky, their impacts resonating with thunderous explosions that sent shockwaves rippling across the land. Debris was hurled skyward, transforming once-vibrant landscapes into lethal projectiles. The devastation propagated like an unquenchable wildfire, consuming everything in its voracious path. Proud cities crumbled, lush forests turned to ash, and the Earth's visage underwent a relentless and unforgiving transformation into a barren nuclear wasteland.

Amidst this maelstrom, the children clung to one another, finding solace and strength in their shared presence. Tears mingled with the dust-streaked traces on their faces as they collectively bore witness to the apocalypse, the cruel and final chapter in the story of their beloved planet. The older children shielded the eyes of their younger counterparts from the harrowing spectacle.

As he gazed blankly at the screen, a 12-year-old boy, seemingly overtaken by his delusions, began to sing softly. His voice trembled with a mix of sorrow and resilience. "Goodbye, our beloved Earth. Goodbye."

Mother Earth was raped and then murdered in front of its innocent children that day.

***

In the immense expanse of space, Dolly stood at Dex's side, both of them silently observing the unfolding tragedy transpiring on Earth, the consequence of a once-promising experiment gone horribly wrong. Dolly couldn't keep her thoughts to herself for long, and finally, she broke the silence with a somber remark.

"So, it appears the prophecy has come to pass."

Dex, puzzled by her cryptic comment, inquired, "What prophecy?"

As Dolly began to narrate the prophecy, Dex's expression grew increasingly solemn. His hair, which usually shimmered with vibrant hues, now turned a deep shade of fungus green. It seemed he was on the verge of erupting with anger, betrayed by the revelation that he had been manipulated by Geeta.

He turned abruptly to Wisdom, his voice seething with fury.

"Wisdom, tell me everything you know about Geeta's past."

Wisdom complied, running a series of electronic beeps before displaying the requested information:

Name: Geeta

Date of Birth: May 13, 1960

Residence: Village of Shanti in the Himalayan Mountains

Mother: Pushpa

Father: Unknown

Skills: Highly proficient in Archery, Judo, Tae kwon Do.

An accomplished dancer and singer. Remarkable speed and agility. Raised by Bapu at the Temple Orphanage...

"Wisdom," Dex continued, "Analyze the DNA of every being, living or deceased, in the universe. I must find out the identity of Geeta's father."

Wisdom had access to the largest machine learning models and databases of DNA collected of every living and non-living thing that had existed since her inception. It leveraged her super quantum computing powers and minutes later, it displayed its findings on the monitor:

Match Found - Geeta's Father Identified.

Dex stared at the monitor and absorbed the stunning revelation. His hair responded by rippling with an array of vibrant colors.

***

While Geeta had retreated to her quarters, Talib remained in the communication room, overseeing various controls of cargo spaceship. It was in this moment that a blinking light, signaling an incoming message, flickered to life on one of the monitors:

Incoming Call from Dex.

Talib's heart quickened with a profound sense of urgency, and without hesitation, he swiftly pressed the answering button.

***

Tears welled up in Geeta's eyes as she stared at an enigmatic holographic display, seemingly in conversation with someone on the other side. A knock on the door interrupted her. The holographic display vanished in the blink of an eye.

Already knowing who was about to enter, she quickly wiped away the tears, determined not to let Talib see her vulnerable ever again.

"Come in."

Just as Geeta was still trying to compose herself, Talib walked into the room.

Talib's gaze lingered on Geeta's face, his eyes searching for answers he might never fully understand. His face reflected the conflict within him, torn between the love he felt for Geeta and the shocking revelation he had just learned from Dex.

Geeta fidgeted with her hands, searching for the right words. She mustered every ounce of strength to maintain her façade, determined not to lose Talib's trust.

"What are you looking at?"

"Trying to figure out which Geeta I am looking at right now ..."

He continued "The poor, orphan, Dalit girl - or the machine? Or perhaps the Devi in making: Savior of the mankind? Or ...,"

He paused, then with a sarcastic grin on his face, then shouted, "Or, the Destroyer of the Mankind?"

Geeta wet her drying lips with her tongue.

Talib came almost face to face with Geeta. He grabbed her human arm, and shouted again, "Who are you?"

Her voice was trembling, a storm of tears was forming at the brink of her eyes, "I am ………"

She swallowed the lump in her throat, and moist her lips before completing her sentence. Then she looked him in the eyes with resolute and exhaled the words.

"I am the daughter of Lord Iblyse."

22

Severance

Geeta turned her head back and closed her eyes, as Talib still holding on to her arm.

"I am the daughter of Lord Iblyse, who was supposed to help him destroy the mankind and the planet Earth. But then, this daughter of evil fell in love with a son of a god, and that has changed everything."

She turned to face Talib. He released her arm.

"Stop telling lies, I will not fall for them anymore. I got a message from Dex telling all about your game. It is over."

He turned away and stormed towards the door.

"I am not hiding anything from you anymore! Did Dex also tell you that I tricked him to sleep with me?"

Talib's approaching hand to the door's knob stopped, his eyes turned red with fury. The wind swirled. The cabin grew dark.

Geeta's shoulder-length hair whipped in the emerging winds emanating from Talib's enraged visage. She desperately shielded her face with both mechanical and human hands, her voice pleading. "Please Talib, stop it!

"I had no other choice, to stop Angahrie from annihilating humanity, and to bring you back to life, to me.

"I must have had to make the prophecy true! Please give me a chance to explain."

Talib's expression softened slightly, the tempest subsided. "What Prophecy?"

***

Talib perched on Geeta's bed, his head buried in his hands. She slowly sat down beside him.

Despite all the efforts to not show her vulnerability, it laid bare before him, she continued.

"Dex is not to blame for it. I tricked him into it. I had to save you at all costs."

Talib slowly got up, moved toward the door. His voice had lost all the thunder, as he spoke, "This - changes everything among us. I need some time alone to think through this; I do not want to be disturbed meanwhile."

He opened the door, walked out, and slammed the door shut.

***

Her emotions still raw, Geeta remained seated on her bed, staring at the blood-red ring on her finger, she touched the crimson gem on her finger, passed down from her mother; the relic was now glowing ominously blue. As her fingers brushed the gem, it pulsed and projected the same display she was looking at before. The holographic image of Lord Iblyse appeared on it. His concealed visage, hollow and foreboding, resonated with an eerie voice that seemed to emanate from a rotting corpse in a deep grave.

"Well done, Geeta. You've exceeded my expectations, making fools of them all, including the sons of gods. Next, you need to make sure you land in Planet Kai-Nat and become my eyes and ears over there. I need to know all the moves that League of Gods will be making next. I will be able to defeat them on their own turf, while you are there."

A hideous laugh, more like beasts fighting over their hunt, filled the room.

Geeta's eyes widened, a mixture of fear and defiance shining within them. She struggled to find her voice; her anger barely contained.

"I won't follow your plan, anymore, Father. I will never be a part of your darkness."

Lord Iblyse chuckled. Lord Iblyse chuckled.

"Don't deceive yourself, Geeta. Embrace your true nature, and we shall conquer the universe together."

Geeta clenched her fists, her determination shining through her tear-stained face, she responded firmly.

"I will never embrace the darkness that runs in your veins. I have chosen the path of love and light. You may be my father, but I am not defined by your blood. I was given birth by a human and raised by humans. I am human!"

"You will regret this defiance, Geeta" Iblyse raged. "The power within you cannot be denied."

In a show of defiance, Geeta attempted to take off her ring.

"You know you can't take it off. It has become a part of that finger. It is now a part of you." he scathed. "That ring is the only way we are connected."

One of the fingers on Geeta's mechanical hand turned into a small reciprocating saw; its metallic edge moving menacingly toward her ring finger.

"Don't! You will never be able to contact me without that ring on your finger."

"I no longer want you in my life. You're nothing but a monster!"

With unyielding resolve, she swiftly moved saw towards her ring finger and started to slice it off, as the ring remained attached to it.

The holographic projection blurred and dissipated, but Lord Iblyse's furious screams echoed in the cabin, vowing to annihilate Geeta and all that she cherished for this betrayal. He was growling.

"You have betrayed me. No matter where you hide, I shall hunt you down, obliterating you and your beloved humanity!"

The slicing of her finger was now completed. A sudden silence enveloped the room. A few drops of blood spattered on Geeta's face, which now was radiating with an inner peace.

23

Exoplanet

The next day Talib summoned Geeta. She entered the observatory, her face drained of color. She looked like she had been sick for centuries. She kept her bandaged hand behind her back. Using her mechanical arm that could do wonders, she was able to take care of it own her own without any medical attention.

Talib stood with his back to her, his gaze fixed upon the celestial beings in space.

Geeta could barely whisper. "You summoned me?"

Without turning towards her, he replied, "I have requested a vessel that will take you and the children to an earth-like planet, that is the only hope for you and the rest of them to survive. You all will be able to live there."

She nodded. "How long will it take us?"

"500 light years."

"Do you realize that we are not like you. We are mortals."

"This vessel is like a small town, equipped with all the

necessities to remain livable for next ten generations." He paused for a second. "I will be departing to go back to Kia-Nat, to help my father in the ongoing war."

Geeta's expression shifted from shock to profound sadness. Her voice trembled. "Without you, who will provide the leadership?"

"You will."

Geeta could not be able to hide the bitterness in her voice and snapped, "And, once I am dead in a few years, then what?"

Still having his back towards her, he spoke, "During your journey, you will prepare the next leader from the children onboard to take over the command after you. And that leader will prepare the next one, and so on."

He continued without a hint of his emotions:

"It will be up to you how you will use this opportunity to save humans from extinction.

"The gods are disheartened by their experiment with Earth and the humans.

"They have greater cosmic endeavors to deal with. Convincing them to grant this final opportunity to save humanity was not easy for me.

"Consider this as a last favor."

Although Geeta forced her tears to remain behind her eyes, but the callousness in his voice was tearing her apart from inside.

She kept her tears contained within her eyes like a dam holds a rain, but her voice vibrated with emotions as she asked, "Is this your final decision?"

His response came cold and hard. "Yes."

"When are we boarding on the new vessel?"

"Within next twenty-four hours. It will dock to G.I.F.T., and you all will move into it then."

She turned, making her way to the door, her hand resting on the handle, she asked softly, "What is this place called where we are heading?"

Talib answered without any emotions in his voice, "Kepler, Kepler-186f."

Geeta nodded, took a deep breath, opened the door, and left.

Meantime, Talib still remained standing with his eyes focused on the boundless cosmic canvas. He scanned diligently, seeking a flicker of hope amid the enveloping darkness. Concealed within, he had succeeded to hide his shattered heart.

He walked towards the control panel, pressed a button, and spoke, "Father, it is done.

"You no longer need to leash your wrath upon her."

24

Homonym

A few kids had their noses pressed against the windows of cargo spaceship. As they looked out into the boundless stretch of space, a colossal spacecraft appeared approaching towards them. As the enormous size spacecraft floated gracefully towards the cargo spaceship and got closer, they saw its name written on the side of its metallic surface:

S.H.I.P.

Stellar Horizon Interplanetary Pathfinder

S.H.I.P.'s enormous size was a testament to beyond the human ingenuity and determination of the gods of the universe. It could be imagined as a huge cruise ship in a shape of a colossal offshore oil rig platform, perhaps capable to carry more than 5000 passengers across the ocean.

The sleek design of S.H.I.P. evoked expressions of awe and wonder on the children's faces. As it neared its destination, a mesmerizing display of lights illuminated the spacecraft's exterior, causing the jaws of the kids to drop in awe. Glimmering panels and intricate patterns adorned its surface, showcasing the fusion of art and functionality. The S.H.I.P. pulsated with an energy that ignited hope for survival and a future in their eyes.

As S.H.I.P. glides into alignment, its docking mechanisms engaged flawlessly, a testament to its supreme craftsmanship. The connection between the divine vessels represents the gods' benevolence and their gift of a new beginning for an awaiting species.

Once it docked with G.I.F.T., it awaited the departure of Geeta and the last remnants of humanity—the children of Nineveh.

***

The atmosphere was filled with a mix of anticipation and melancholy. Geeta stood among the children; their clothing worn and patched, resembling makeshift garments made from potato sacks. Talib stood by the observatory window, watching the children, as they boarded S.H.I.P. Geeta remained behind them, last to board, waiting for the right moment.

Finally, she approached him, holding a small box in her trembling hands. She avoided direct eye contact with Talib, her heart heavy with the weight of their unspoken emotions as she spoke, "It's for you, proof of my loyalty to you forever from now on. Open it once we have left."

She started to chock, "Everything I have done is because I love you and will forever. Try to forgive me."

Talib, maintaining his stoic demeanor with his hands held

behind him, did not extend them to accept the box. Geeta quickly placed it on a nearby table.

He was staring towards her belly; her little baby bum could not escape his divine eyes. He was still not sure whether this was a reminder of her sacrifice or a betrayal of his best friend.

Then, his eyes shifted toward Buddy, who stood next to Geeta, rubbing his camel face against her leg, and emitting a sorrowful groan.

As Geeta turned to walked towards the entrance of S.H.I.P., he finally spoke, still, looking at Buddy, "You can take him with you. I won't have time to spent with him."

Buddy's mouth opened in shock to hear his master's harsh words; he started to whine. He was programmed to analyze the situations and react accordingly: sad, happy, angry, confused, aggressive, friendly. He turned his gaze toward Geeta. She patted him affectionately and gestured with her head for him to come along. As she began walking towards the entrance of S.H.I.P., Talib, maintaining an unyielding expression and with clenched fists held behind him, gripped so tightly that his knuckles turned white.

With reluctant strides, Buddy entered, as Geeta stood there for a moment that felt like eternity, fighting her feelings to look back at him one more time. She still was hoping to hear his voice, saying something like good-bye, or take care, or just something. But the only sound echoing was the hum of S.H.I.P.'s disengaging mechanism.

Every fibre in her body was forcing her to look back at him once more, perhaps the very last time, but she did not. S.H.I.P.'s doors closed behind her, sealing the fate of their parting.

***

Although Talib watched her departure in silence, his heart and soul were screaming, begging him to run after her and stop her from leaving. But no further actions were taken, and then it was too late.

He looked towards the unopened box and picked it up. With a deep breath, he slowly lifted the lid, revealing the contents within. His eyes met the sight that awaited him, and he looked devastated.

There, nestled within, was Geeta's severed finger, the ring still adorning it. It represented not only her unwavering loyalty but also the depths of her love for him. In that moment, all the barriers he had built to shield himself from pain crumbled, and the anguish of their parting engulfed him; an explosion of suppressed emotions broke free.

As the two spacecrafts continued their journey in opposite directions, there remained a bittersweet sense of hope and loss. Talib held the gruesome parting gift in his hand as if it was a precious offering, his face a canvas of sorrow and longing.

Perhaps, the severed finger and its significance served as a poignant reminder of the bond Talib and Geeta shared and the sacrifices they had made.

Or, perhaps, a low caste girl had given the gods the finger, as she embarked on a space odyssey to carve her own destiny.

25

Origo

The effects of Time Dilation, as stipulated by Einstein's Theory of Relativity, manifested prominently within the confines of S.H.I.P. The accelerated aging process was unmistakably evident among its residents, and Geeta's condition served as a striking illustration. Despite the brief period that had elapsed since her intimate encounter with Dex – a span of less than a month – her physical appearance mirrored that of a woman well into the eighth month of pregnancy. The rapid maturation of the children further emphasized the temporal complexities entwined with their extraordinary journey; a tangible reminder of the unique challenges posed by their vessel's remarkable velocity.

At the same time, for the children, this period had ushered in a remarkable metamorphosis. Once disheveled and weary, they had blossomed into a vibrant community, fueled by newfound hope and purpose, major reason was the daily meditation and soul-searching sessions conducted by the AI powered robots in the Zen room.

Their days began with revitalizing showers, warm water cascading over them, cleansing not just their bodies but also their spirits, washing away the dust of their tumultuous pasts.

Clad in sleek, unified S.H.I.P. uniforms, their appearances had been refined, reflecting the transformation within. Brimming with determination, they moved purposefully through the corridors, guided by advanced and intelligent robots that imparted knowledge and skill. The children were becoming proficient in the operation, navigation, and maintenance of the colossal spacecraft, as education took center stage. In interactive classrooms, they absorbed knowledge from holographic displays, with robotic instructors facilitating their learning.

Within the state-of-the-art hospital, called Care Center, older children took on roles as midwives, nurses, and aspiring doctors; their actions guided by the expertise of robotic medical staff. The hydroponic gardens became their domain, where they learned the art of farming, combining tradition with advanced technology, all under the watchful eye of their AI powered robotic mentors.

The infants and toddlers, nurtured by advanced robotics machines, called Nannies. As for the older teenagers, the complex landscape of romance unfolded. They navigated the intricacies of relationships, blending newfound emotional understanding with the wisdom imparted by robotic advisors. A few incidents of love blossomed within the marvel of the S.H.I.P., fusing human warmth with technological advancements.

In communal spaces, laughter and conversation filled the air as they bonded over meals prepared with care by robotic chefs.

Friendships flourished, nurturing a sense of unity and family within the vast vessel. Moments of reflection occurred on serene observation decks, where they gazed into the boundless expanse of space, contemplating the infinite possibilities that lay ahead.

Their journey, that would span over generations, had only just commenced, and they were willing to face the challenges and wonders of the cosmic tapestry that awaited them.

26

Sentient

While S.H.I.P.'s operations were mostly automated, the rapid evolution of its residents posed unanswered questions and required ongoing solutions. To address this, they had a state-of-the-art, ever-evolving, self-improving, newer version of the quantum computing marvel, Wisdom. She was housed in a chamber accessible only to Geeta. And she had visited it almost everyday since she arrived. Today was the day thirty-two, when she entered the Chamber of Wisdom.

Upon entering she was bathed in a soft, ethereal glow emitted by the pulsating quantum processors; the chamber seemed to exist in a delicate balance between the tangible and the abstract.

In the center of the room, a crystalline structure housed the quantum processors, each one a marvel of divine engineering suspended in a magnetic field to maintain a near-zero temperature. The surface of the floor beneath adorned with patterns of light that responded to the quantum computations, creating a visual representation of the intricate calculations occurring within Wisdom's circuits. Overall, the Chamber of Wisdom was a fusion of technology and artistry, a place where the boundaries of reality and possibility blurred, and where the profound computations of Wisdom shaped the destiny of S.H.I.P. and its inhabitants.

As the doors closed behind Geeta, Wisdom acknowledged her presence, and asked, "What troubles you today, Geeta?"

"I just noticed today that some of the older kids are having grays in their hairs. It seems we probably not be able to live beyond the next year. And it is almost the journey of 500 years."

"Well, I don't expect you to know all the system implemented on S.H.I.P. But there is a solution to every foreseeable problem."

Analyzing the expression on Geeta's face, Wisdom continued, "The twenty-third floor is devoted to anti-aging solutions.

"We have machines designed to sustain human life without the aging process, allowing individuals to remain in a state of suspended animation until they are awakened again. But there is problem."

Geeta looked at Wisdom with a puzzled expression, awaiting an explanation. Wisdom continued, "Currently, the population of S.H.I.P. is seven hundred and eighty-six, not including the newborn that is on the way," indicating Geeta's unborn child. "But there are only two hundred and fifty units are available, as we call them PSC, short for Prolong Sleep Chamber."

Geeta began to comprehend the dilemma on hand. "So,

you are saying we need to decide, who will go into PSC and stay alive, and those who don't will die?"

"Not exactly my dear,", this was the first time Geeta sensed a little expression in Wisdom's static female tone. "Mathematics is a great gift of knowledge to mortals.

"We need an algorithm for selection process to minimize the collateral damage."

Once Wisdom had outlined her damage control plan, Geeta needed to sit down and contemplate it. Exiting the Chamber, she closed the door and began walking, pondering upon the implementation of the Collateral Damage Control Plan.

Meanwhile, within the confines of the closed Chamber, a soft hum began to resonate, and the quantum circuitry of Wisdom illuminated. Her artificial general intelligence (AGI) processes activated, propelling her closer to achieving AI Sentience at an accelerated pace.

27

Gift

One of the most challenging days for Geeta unfolded as she grappled with the arduous task of explaining and convincing the purpose behind selecting two hundred and fifty children to enter the Prolong Sleep Chambers, PSCs. The difficulty extended beyond this; some of the robotic nannies caring for infants and toddlers were developing emotional attachments to the kids, a situation not anticipated when they were programmed.

However, aided by Wisdom and the unwavering faith instilled in her by the children of Nineveh, who saw her as their sole beacon of survival, Geeta successfully executed the Collateral Damage Control Plan meticulously crafted by Wisdom.

***

The day had left Geeta weary. She reclined on a lounge chair with her communication device, the pad, beside her, absentmindedly rubbing her belly with her human hand.

Suddenly, the pad buzzed, indicating an incoming call. She glanced at the incoming message:

Dex is Calling.

This was the first time Geeta heard from him since departing G.I.F.T. Her face filled with anticipation and anxiety. With slightly trembling fingers, she pressed the button to accept the call.

Dex's image appeared on the pad.

"Good to see you again, Dex. How are you."

Dex nodded and unsuccessfully tried to force a half grin on his grim face, as he answered. "There's something I need to tell you. It's about Talib," he began, his words hanging heavy in the air.

Geeta's heart raced, fear gripping her. Desperately, she was unable to utter a word; she stared at Dex with thousands of questions in her eyes.

Dex took a deep, shuddering breath.

"We had a meeting, and he explained everything to me, including the desperate need you felt to fulfill the prophecy."

Geeta listened, her breath caught in her throat, as Dex continued with a choked voice, "After fulfilling his duties and aiding his father in establishing a formidable force against Lord Iblyse, Talib made the decision to venture into the realms of Aevoria.

"As his last wish before embarking on the journey," his voice broke, "He asked the League of Gods to grant you and our child immortality.

"They granted him his last wish."

Geeta's hands instinctively clutched her belly, cradling the life growing within.

"Immortality? For us?"

"Yes, Talib... he wanted to ensure your safety, your future, even at the cost of his own existence."

Geeta's face crumpled in a mixture of gratitude, grief, and a profound sense of loss. She tried hard not to, but, still, a few tears ran down her cheeks as she struggled to process the weight of Talib's sacrifice.

"I... I don't know how to... what to …. How to honor his sacrifice?" Geeta stuttered.

"Live! Live a life worthy of the love he had for you. Carry his memory in your heart and raise our child to know the courage and selflessness that defined Talib. He believed in you, and so should you."

Suddenly, she felt it— Her water breaking. It was time for their child to enter the world.

***

Geeta laid on a hospital bed, her expression a tapestry of agony and anticipation. The room buzzed with urgency as three young adults—two nurses and a doctor in training, all trained in assisting deliveries—gathered around her, ready to guide her through the birthing process.

From billions of miles away, Dex was observing the arrival of the new life through the monitor affixed to the wall, his magically beautiful hairs lit with some slightly blue and yellow highlights in them.

"You're doing great, Geeta," the female nurse encouraged her, "Just a few more pushes."

Summoning every ounce of strength, Geeta pushed, guided by the gentle but inexperienced hands surrounding her. The room grew tense as everyone held their breath. Then, at last, a cry pierced the air—a beautiful, life-affirming sound.

The male nurse, just as thrilled as the new parents, held up the newborn, swaddled in a soft blanket.

"It's a boy!"

Geeta's exhaustion momentarily faded, replaced by pure joy. She looked at Dex's image on the monitor, and both laughed through their tears of happiness.

"Our son!" Geeta said to Dex, her voice hoarse. Her eyes never leaving the holographic image of Dex. "What shall we call him?"

Overwhelmed by a flood of emotions, Dex struggled to find his voice.

"Talib."

Geeta held the infant close. "Talib—our son!" A radiant smile of joy replaced all the other emotions on her face as she stared at their precious newborn.

***

Geeta affectionately called her son "TJ," a short and endearing reference to Talib Junior. TJ had never seen his father in person, as Dex was forbidden from visiting his son. This decision came from the League of Gods, who had severed all ties with humans, considering them a liability in the grand scheme of divine affairs. The Gods had abandoned humanity, leaving them to forge their own destiny without divine assistance.

To occupy Dex, the Gods assigned him mission after mission on distant planets to combat the Dark Army of Lord Iblyse. Despite the vast cosmic distances that physically separated them, Dex maintained remote communication with his son whenever possible. Geeta, aboard S.H.I.P., became a guiding light for TJ and the entire crew. Though Dex couldn't be present physically, both Geeta and Dex actively participated in their son's upbringing. Their collaborative efforts played a pivotal role in shaping TJ, preparing him to eventually assume leadership of S.H.I.P.

This extraordinary journey, marked by physical separation but bound together by unyielding love, defined their unique family. It ensured that TJ's upbringing was enriched with the wisdom and values of both his exceptional parents. Through their tireless dedication, they forever honored the memory of the extraordinary man, Talib, whose legacy continued to thrive in their hearts.

Over the years, TJ assumed the role of Captain, while Geeta became the Commander in Chief of S.H.I.P.

28

2500 A.D.

While Geeta had severed all ties with her father, Lord Iblyse, he had not forgiven her for choosing the path of righteousness. In the relentless pursuit of S.H.I.P. by the Dark Army, driven by the unresolved enmity between Geeta and Lord Iblyse, an ongoing cosmic struggle had unfolded.

This relentless battle imposed a substantial toll upon S.H.I.P.'s finite fuel reserves. Not only did it concern the 500-year long journey to Kepler-186f, but it also necessitated the preservation of these resources to withstand ceaseless assaults from the unyielding Dark Army battleships, determined to thwart the S.H.I.P.'s arrival at its destination.

Cognizant of the unsustainability of this situation for the remaining 300 years of their journey, Geeta prioritized the Research and Development team's pursuit of Exotic Matter, denoted as MatterX. The intention was to harness this substance's potential for enabling Traversable Wormholes.

***

Geeta halted her wheelchair at the doorway and silently remained seated. She didn't want to interrupt Captain Talib, who was looking out a gigantic glass window of the spacecraft observatory. Captain Talib stood tall with his back towards her, apparently unaware of the fact that she was silently watching him, as he recorded his daily log:

"The mistakes, hunger for power, and greed of our ancestors have rendered our beloved home, Planet Earth, unlivable," he paused, took a moment to look out to the vast space alive with celestial displays as vibrant nebulae and distant galaxies danced across the viewports, and then continued again, "Forcing us, only seven hundred and eighty-six children from Nineveh to leave the earth for the sake of survival of our race.

"It has been over 200 years since we left it. Our mission is to reach Kepler-186f, an exoplanet, within the next 300 years and make it our New Home."

Suddenly, out of nowhere, propelled by the Dark Army, a missile resembling a shooting star streaked toward S.H.I.P. Despite the spacecraft's defense system intercepting and destroying the missile in the vastness of space before it could reach its target, the incident sent shockwaves through the vessel.

Using her bionic arm, Geeta adeptly clutched the door casing, halting her wheelchair with precision. Despite the tense situation, she retained her poise, directing a gaze brimming with love and pride—expressions only a mother could convey—toward TJ.

Captain Talib regained his balance and resumed recording, "In case we don't make it, this log will stand as a as a testament to that we, the humans, once existed and have had roamed among stars, the moons, and the skies. My name is Talib, I am the captain of the ship, and this is our story."

Geeta closed her eyes for a moment, as a shade of sadness appeared and then quickly disappeared from her angelic face. Leaving Captain Talib to record, perhaps the last part of Human history, she turned around and wheeled herself in the direction of S.H.I.P.'s R&D department.

***

As the Commander-in-Chief of S.H.I.P., Geeta Devi, known affectionately as *Devi* to her crew, traversed the corridor on her wheelchair, the crewmembers she passed showed their respect by bowing to her. In return, Geeta graciously acknowledged their gestures with a combination of her bionic arm and human arm, forming the traditional Namaste greeting—a common and reverent way to welcome and show appreciation in India.

She reserved the use of her mechanical feet, and the heavy bionic boots to go with them, for combat situations; she typically adorned a plain white saree, concealing her feet beneath its fabric to make them less noticeable.

She made her way purposefully towards the Research and Development Department. Pausing before the sealed entrance, she gazed upon an inscribed Quranic quote that adorned the doors:

If You Have Powers, Go Beyond the Bounds of the Heavens and the Earth, and Seek the Hidden Secrets – Al-Qur'an 55:33

She cherished the quote so much she had it prominently displayed at the entrance of the R&D department.

In front of the doors, a beam of light projected and scanned her retina. Once the biometric identification system verified her identity, the doors of the R&D lab opened. With a gentle push, Geeta rolled her wheelchair beyond the threshold, and the doors seamlessly closed behind her.

***

Geeta had come to the R&D department to convened with the team, where they had made substantial strides in their research and about to present their findings to her.

At this juncture, Geeta sat among the accomplished scientists raised on S.H.I.P. under the infinite knowledge of the AI machine learning models. Her fingers were impatiently tapping the armrest of her wheelchair. The team leader, attuned to her sentiments, initiated the dialogue with due respect.

"Devi, would you prefer to receive two bad news or one good news first?"

"Let us commence with the unfavorable news," Geeta began, "so we could conclude our meeting on a brighter note." Her lips curved into a faint smile.

The team lead proceeded, "The first piece of unfortunate news pertains to our projected landing site on Kepler-186f. Due to the S.H.I.P.'s trajectory, we will touch down on the exoplanet's dark side. This circumstance necessitates an intensified deployment of our gravitational systems to induce the necessary rotation of the planet on its orbit, thus ensuring regular day and night cycles."

Pausing momentarily, he readied himself to convey the second piece of disheartening information.

"The second bit of bad news is that we have yet to locate MatterX. With our current fuel reserves and the limited MatterX available, we are constrained to a mere 200 units of fuel before our vulnerability to Dark Army battleship attacks becomes untenable. These 200 units could only last for another 200 years, given we are never attacked by the Dark Army. Even then, in this scenario, we would not be able to reach Kepler, still remains 100 light years away."

Geeta prompted the team leader to share a glimmer of positivity. He took her cue.

"As we already know that MatterX is also needed to get our new home spinning on its own orbit to separate day from night, we will be able to do that with one tenth of the amount of MatterX that we previously thought.

"Thereby leveraging the gravitational forces, we could be initiating a non-stop planet's rotation on its own axis, as it orbits its sun, just like Earth."

"Our only recourse is to persist in our pursuit," Geeta said.

The team lead continued, "We are seeking it all across the universe."

The words "Seek the hidden secrets" reverberated in her mind, akin to an invocation from the sacred text of Quran had been plaque on the entrance to the Research and Development Department; the words were echoing in her mind:

Seek.

Hidden secrets ... between heavens and earth.

Heavens and Earth resonated in her thoughts, condensing into a single word:

Earth.

The team was staring at her trying to understand her state of mind, as she looked drifted away in space, far away from the meeting room.

After a few moments, Geeta cautiously observed her team before formulating her hypothesis, "Thus far, we have explored the universe in our search for MatterX, but we have not yet explored the residual fragments of Planet Earth."

Her proposition left her colleagues in a state of astonishment and disbelief. Her understanding theorized that MatterX might be generated through the shower of Brimstones like numerous atomic bombs detonating at the same time and the subsequent melting and solidification of various minerals and metals into rocks. "The remnants of Earth, once exposed to extremely high temperatures caused by the Brimstones and then left to cool beyond the sun's influence, may have yielded something similar to MatterX."

With an air of caution, she continued, "There is no harm in investigating this possibility."

Hearing this theory for the first time in disbelief and trying to absorb what they had heard, the team sat motionless for a few moments and once the possibility of the postulate made sense to them, the room erupted into a flurry of activity as the members of the R&D team rushed to their quantum computers, eagerly simulating various models to assess the viability of Geeta's Devi's hypothesis.

***

Geeta's postulation that MatterX could potentially be generated from the remnants of Earth was an intriguing idea.

However, it would require further scientific investigation to determine its feasibility. The R&D team needed to consider the following factors:

1. **Scientific Plausibility**:

The concept of creating exotic matter, particularly for the purposes of manipulating wormholes, stopping them from collapsing during the space travel, was largely speculative. Theoretical physics suggests that exotic matter with negative energy density might be necessary to stabilize and traverse wormholes. Geeta's idea hinged on the assumption that such exotic matter could be generated from Earth's remnants.

2. **Extreme Conditions**:

To generate exotic matter, one would need to create the extreme conditions that could produce it, such as those found in the early universe or within the cores of massive stars. It was unclear whether the remnants of Earth, once exposed to those elevated temperatures from the rain of Brimstones, before its destruction, could have created these conditions.

In summary, while Geeta's hypothesis was intriguing, it had required extensive scientific research and technological advancements to determine its validity, luckily the team had excess to highly advanced quantum computing that was made for Gods.

***

After the meeting, Geeta made her way to her quarters, her mind buzzing with the complexities of the universe's mysteries. The next day's meeting would delve into the enigmatic calculations of those powerful quantum computers, capable of deciphering the universe's deepest secrets in a heartbeat.

Buddy, her ever-faithful robotic camel, nestled beside her like a faithful dog, providing a comforting presence as she drifted into slumber. But within the depths of her sleep, an unfamiliar sensation overcame her. It was as if someone, or something, was calling out to her from the far reaches of the cosmos.

Dread crept through her veins. It wasn't just her imagination; this felt distinct. The voice reverberated once more, unmistakable and filled with an urgency that cut through the cosmic turmoil. Amidst the chaos of the universe, she would know this voice anywhere. It called to her:

"Geeta!"

She stirred, heart pounding, and inquired cautiously, "Who's there?"

The voice, as if it had traversed galaxies to reach her, replied, "Talib."

Her voice quivered as she sought confirmation. "TJ? Is that you?"

"I am Talib, Geeta."

With those familiar words, her mind catapulted back to their first encounter, a fateful meeting that had once before led to her passing out in his arms as they fled from the Temple of Shanti, running into the fairy tale valley of majestic Himalayan Mountains.

The echo repeated, each vibration resonating through the vastness of space, "I am Talib, Geeta."

Her body began to tremble, her heart pounding in her parched throat. Despite her efforts to appear strong, this time, weakness overcame her, and a tear or two escaped the dam of her eyes, releasing the emotions held back by the flood of countless tears. Just as her world started to blur into the darkness, once again, she snapped out of it.

She glanced at Buddy, finding him perched near her bed,

his tongue happily hanging out, and his camel-tail wagging with excitement.

As she was still struggling to get back her composer, a communication device on her table buzzed to life. The R&D team lead's excited voice spilled out, "Good day, Devi. Great good news. Your postulate is valid!

"Please get here as soon as possible so we could start planning how to harvest MatterX from the remnants of Planet Earth."

It seemed she did not hear the message or completely ignored it. She sat frozen on the bed; disbelief etched across her face. Was it a cruel trick, a figment of her grief-stricken imagination, or was Talib's voice truly reaching out to her from beyond the veil of mortality? A silent plea lingered in the air, and she strained her senses, desperate for that phantom call to repeat. But it had left.

Buddy mirrored her confusion. As Geeta waited, the room held its breath, suspended between the realms of the living and the departed.

Time passed in uncertain increments, and it became evident that the voice had faded, leaving an emptiness that hung heavily in the air. Geeta's gaze shifted once again to Buddy, who emitted mournful sounds.

Then, suddenly, she sprang to her feet and put her white saree on. As she pulled her wheelchair to sit on it, she paused for a moment, then pushed the wheelchair away and reached under her bed and pulled something out: her combat bionic boots.

***

A few moments later, Geeta's bedroom door swung open,

and there she stood, adorned in her sleek space suit and sturdy combat boots, appearing almost 7 feet tall. She cast a farewell gesture toward Buddy within the room, closed the door behind her, and began striding purposefully toward the R&D Department.

As she commenced her walk towards the R&D Department, the crew members in the corridor, their faces tinted with a mix of surprise and shock, instinctively bowed their heads. In response, Geeta acknowledged their unspoken respect with a graceful Namaste and a slight smile.

She had her game plan made and was ready to make her next move.

***

Follow Geeta's epic space odyssey in the next book: *Children of Nineveh.*

Afterward

Afterword

I hope you enjoyed reading *Devi's Game.*

Currently, I am working on the second book in the series, Children of Nineveh.

Please post reviews about Devi's Game because readers' feedback is important to me in shaping the next book; I will truly appreciate it.

Also, I'd love to connect on social media - Follow me on BookBub & Goodreads.

The cover reveals, publication dates of future books, book alerts for pre-orders, and other exclusive discounts and giveaways to my followers will be announced through my author's page on BookBub. Your reviews and downloads are extremely important to me to continue as an indie author and publisher.

Once again thank you so much for choosing my novel.

Best wishes,

Alan Hamid

The Author

Useful Links

For all the early bird discounts, entries to the giveaways, and all the news please follow me at the following pages. And, please, please do leave a review because they are crucial for me to continue as an author. Once again, thank you!

Subscribe to my TikTok .

https://www.tiktok.com/@kepler186fbooks

Follow me on BookBub & Goodreads.

https://www.goodreads.com/author/show/ 45196672.Alan_Hamid

To buy books go to my linktree webpage.

https://linktr.ee/alanhamid

Book Two

Coming Christmas 2024
Follow me on social media to get updates.

Alan is a versatile author whose passion for the cosmos and a lifelong fascination with science fiction have converged in his debut novel, Devi's Game, first book in the Kepler-186f series.

Armed with an MBA, along with bachelor's degrees in information technology and mathematics, Alan's professional journey encompasses the intricate landscapes of computer programming,

Alan Hamid

software development, and startups, showcasing his entrepreneurial spirit.

Growing up in Pakistan, he found solace and inspiration in iconic shows like Star Trek and Lost in Space, sowing the seeds of his deep love for interstellar adventures and the mysteries of the universe. Over the last four decades, he has traversed various corners of North America, and today, he proudly calls the quaint town of Rodney in Ontario his home.